Illusion of Life

KC Burn

This revised work was first published as Trompe L'oeil by Loose Id in 2011.

ISBN-13: 978-0-9981807-2-4

DEDICATION

As always, I couldn't do this without the support of the hubby, Alex, and my super support posse - Dottie, Chudney, Book Club, Tara, ZAM, Lex. A special thanks to Dolorianne who helped me brainstorm a new title for this book.

Thanks also to all those many, many authors who've given me advice on self-publishing - your help has been invaluable. There are too many to list, but I definitely have to give a shout out to B.a. Tortuga and Julia Talbot who sat through the Skype call of minutiae..

CHAPTER ONE

Tyler Williams's sister bounded into his apartment with a sickening cheerfulness, considering he and his best friend, Craig, had been hauling boxes and furniture for the past eight hours in the sweltering heat. The A/C window units were taking a damn long time to start working, although Ty hadn't bothered turning them on until they were almost finished moving.

Mandy's glossy black hair was normally tamed, but the humidity had it swirling about her head in reckless waves, much like Ty's own did on a daily basis. Most people thought they were twins, but Mandy was three years older than his almost thirty.

"Hi guys." Mandy swiped Ty's beer from his hand and took a swig.

"Hey!" Ty tried to take the bottle back but Mandy danced out of the way. "There's more beer in the fridge."

"Then go get one." Mandy stuck her tongue out at him.

"So help me, sis, you do that again and I'll grab that tongue," Ty threatened as he walked the short distance to his new kitchen. This apartment suited him much better than his previous modern suburban atrocity. In spite of the weird dimensions from cutting one old house into six apartments, he loved his new place. For a change, he could now walk to work or the subway, and he'd never have to drive in the winter again. The place was perfect.

"Ooh. I'm so scared."

"Bring me another one, Ty," Craig called out.

Ty smirked and handed bottles around, having anticipated the request. Craig, a big, sexy Italian cop, had been his best friend since grade school, and Ty knew what he wanted. If the man weren't straight, he'd be perfect.

Mandy leaned down and kissed Craig on the cheek. "How are ya, big boy?"

Craig shrugged. "Same old, same old."

"Okay, Tyler, show me around, quick-quick, because I got you the best housewarming present. Although this house doesn't exactly need any more warming. Did you get a break on the rent because your apartment's in hell?"

Craig snorted from his corner of Ty's brand-new couch. "Air-conditioning, my ass. June's too fucking hot to move."

"I just turned on the A/C a few minutes ago. And I wasn't going to break my lease just for you, Craig." Ty turned a mock glare on both of them. The truth was, sticking it out until the end of his lease had been monstrously difficult. Preston had fucked him in every room and on every surface, before finally fucking him over. By Christmas, everything had gone to shit, and he'd wanted to run. He was no longer in love with Preston, if he ever had been, but the memories of his foolishness were hard to handle.

"Can you pop down to my car and bring up Tyler's housewarming present?" Mandy dangled her car keys at Craig.

Warmth spread in Ty's chest. They might torment each other like any other siblings, but he and Mandy had always been close. She'd stuck by him when his parents hadn't, but he still hadn't expected a housewarming gift.

"What does it look like?" Craig asked.

"You won't be able to miss it." Mandy pasted on her version of a mysterious smile. Ty reminded himself to avoid that one—it made her look like a demented imp, and might look similar on him.

This better not be a setup. His sister had super-shitty taste in gay men. 'Course, so did he, as evidenced by Preston. They probably shared a genetic defect.

"So, show me the place. I want to see the den of loving." Mandy waved her hands imperiously.

"The what?" Ty knew he shouldn't ask, but if he didn't, Craig would as soon as he stopped choking on his beer.

"Hey, when you signed the lease on this place, the master bedroom was all you could talk about. I figured you were planning on hosting crazy orgies or buying a sex slave or something."

Blood rushed to his cheeks. Mandy was the crazy one, judging from her extremely uncensored stories, which had gotten even more graphic after she married Craig's partner on the force. Jake would have been helping with the move too, but he'd dislocated his shoulder a week ago in a tussle with a suspect and couldn't do any heavy lifting.

"A sex slave?" Craig finally caught his breath. "Yeah, that sounds like our Tyler." The sarcastic tone was a bit insulting.

Were they saying he was repressed? He'd had a boyfriend and his share of one-night stands. So what if his share could be counted on one hand? He was single, one hundred percent out of the closet, and ready for lots of sex—as soon as he got up the courage to go out and get some.

"Why are you both picking on me?"

"Mmm, just because you're you, little bro. C'mon. Show me the sex cave."

Ty let loose a chuckle. Sex cave. That had a nice ring to it.

After a quick tour, they stood in the master bedroom.

"Oh my God, Ty, this place is awesome! I thought it was weird you weren't making the second bedroom into an office, but you've got tons of room here. And when you mentioned a whirlpool tub, I thought you were talking about a bathtub with jets. You could swim laps in that damn thing. I'm insanely jealous. Put a fridge in here, and you won't have to let your sex slave out of this room for days."

"Shut up about the sex slave!" Embarrassment colored his laugh because it was true. Find the right man, and they wouldn't have to leave for anything except to eat. Stupidly, the romantic idea that the apartment was designed for a couple had been the deciding factor for taking the apartment. But how could he trust another man after Preston? Love 'em and leave 'em—that was safer for his heart.

"This is perfect. I can't believe how awesome my gift will look in here."

"I can take a hint." Craig left, jingling Mandy's car keys.

"Modest much, Mandy?" Inside, Ty was quaking. She hadn't gotten him a prostitute, had she? Was that what all the sex-slave talk was about? Shit. He wasn't ready. Not for the one-night stands he hoped to have, not for a paid date. Nothing. He hadn't had sex since...well...since weeks before his breakup with that cheating bastard.

"Hey, when you're as good as I am, modesty is just a ridiculous lie." Mandy grinned at him.

"Uh-huh. Let's see it. It better be good." It also better not be a man, or he was going to kill his sister. He was sweaty and hot, and his hair was plastered to his head. None of which did a thing for his self-confidence.

Ty flopped down on his bare mattress and thought about looking for sheets. Nah, he didn't have the energy right now.

"Seriously, how are you doing?" Mandy perched on the edge of the mattress next to him.

"I'm okay. Great apartment, great job."

She inspected his face as though searching for a lie. He wasn't lying, much. But it had been over six months since his life fell apart, and he was getting tired of reassuring people.

Craig's heavy tread alerted them to his return, and Ty wanted to see what Mandy had gotten him, if only to keep her from looking at him with that pitying expression.

Ty sat up as Craig wrestled an enormous rectangular package wrapped in brown paper into the bedroom.

"Holy shit, sis. It's bigger than Craig." No exaggeration—it had to be six and a half feet long, and Craig was only six foot one. Nor was it some random man his sister thought he should hook up with. "What is it?"

Mandy ignored him as she peered at the wall beside the bed. "Here. Right here." She pointed, talking to Craig.

"Here, what?" they both asked in unison.

"Hang it here. It's perfect."

Craig propped the package against the wall and retreated, presumably to locate Ty's toolbox.

"Let me see." Anticipation was making Ty twitchy. Mandy slapped his hand as he reached for the paper covering.

"Just wait. It'll be like one of those fancy unveilings."

"Uh-huh. Right." Ty fell back on the bed while Craig began measuring and hammering. "So, you got me a painting? What is it? Paint by numbers? Black velvet? One that only shows its best features under black light?"

"Shut up, Tyler. Just wait a few more minutes, okay?"

Ty shut up. As long as it wasn't a picture of a six-foot-tall clown, it didn't matter much what it was.

Finally the painting was hung to Mandy's satisfaction. Craig sat down beside him on the bed while Mandy reached dramatically for the brown paper cover.

"I give you Maxwell Friedland." She ripped the paper away, leaving Ty speechless.

"Holy shit," Craig muttered beside him.

The man in the painting was breathtaking. Ty didn't know a lot about painting, but he didn't think he'd seen one as lifelike, almost like a photograph. The mop of blond hair, highlighted with honey and gold, looked soft and real enough to run his fingers through. The bright blue eyes glowed like star sapphires. Tyler's cock flexed slightly, and his face flushed between the conflicts of lust and embarrassment. Lust whispered in his ear that the "painting" was hung to Tyler's satisfaction and then some. He wasn't aware artists painted life-sized portraits of naked men who were...blatantly aroused.

Ty found his voice. "Mandy, what the hell?"

"Isn't he gorgeous? What better way to celebrate your new life?"

Ty bit his lip. He understood Mandy's motivation. He was finally out—to everyone—and it was a relief not to hide anymore. But the process of coming out had been painful and humiliating. Hell, this way he'd never have to announce it again. Anyone who saw this painting would know.

Craig shook his head and downed the last of his beer.

As Ty gazed at the spectacular specimen, he sensed Mandy's mood deflating.

"You don't like it?"

"No, Mandy, it...he is gorgeous. It's a great way to celebrate. You said

Maxwell...Friedland? Is he the painter?"

"Nope." Mandy's smile returned full force. "Maxwell is the man in the painting. It's a stunning picture, isn't it?" Mandy's tone was self-congratulatory, like she'd painted the damn thing herself.

"Yes, but that's not what's got you all hyped." Ty knew his sister well. "Why is he so sad?"

The more Ty looked at the painting, the more he sensed despair, the hopelessness of the subject. Maxwell appeared to be in his early to mid-thirties and had the kind of physique Ty drooled over on construction workers and firefighters.

"Sad?" Craig scoffed. "If that dude were any happier, the painting would be in 3-D poking your eye out."

"He looks quite happy to me too." Mandy smirked and drew her finger along the impressive erection.

Ty grabbed her wrist and pulled her away from the painting. "Mandy, cut it out!"

The strange surge of anger came out of nowhere, but if it was his painting now, he'd have some say about who touched it.

"Possessive already? I love it. Anyway, like I said, I don't think he's sad, but there's definitely a mystery surrounding old Maxwell here."

"A mystery?" He glanced over at the bookshelf destined to contain his collection of mystery novels. Damn. His sister knew him as well as he knew her. Craig sat up a little straighter beside him.

"Historical mystery—right up your alley."

Hmph. Well, maybe. Even if his field was medieval Europe, not twentieth-century artwork. "What's the mystery?"

"You know I've been hoping to get the Victor Cranston estate, right?" Mandy's business was finding art and antiques for her shop and she'd been salivating over Cranston's estate, repeatedly bitching about the contested will, since the man had died six years ago. "Well, the estate's finally cleared, and the heirs agreed to let me broker the sale. But this particular piece is a bit of an embarrassment for everyone. It seems that Uncle Victor was gay and quite flagrant about it."

"Congrats, but so what if Uncle Victor was gay? It's not a bad thing." Ty frowned. He was sympathetic to the lack of familial tolerance. Just look at his own parents.

Mandy smacked his bicep, and he howled in fake agony. Craig was left to play peacemaker. "Okay, kids, knock it off."

Mandy glared at both of them before she continued. "No, being gay and open is not a bad thing, Tyler, but the estate had to pay off half a dozen harassment suits in the final years of Uncle Victor's life. The heirs had a hard time keeping publicity down, and this painting represents the pinnacle of the Cranston scandal, even though it happened in the thirties."

"And? Were any of those heirs even alive at the time? Why do they care that Cranston kept a painting of his lover?" Because there was no doubt in Ty's mind that Maxwell was Cranston's lover.

"Well, the painting is a little over the top, don't you think?" Mandy asked. "After all, not everyone would want this around. Not even these days, never mind eighty-ish years ago."

But somehow his sister thought he did. She wasn't exactly wrong, but what did that say about him?

"Go on."

"Anyway, Maxwell was one of the artists Victor Cranston sponsored during the Depression. When he mysteriously disappeared, most people believed Victor killed him for sleeping with another man, but the police were never able to prove anything. The heirs wanted to destroy the painting rather than having the speculation resume at auction, but I convinced them to let me have it, on the condition it didn't go to auction. I paid them a fair price, and they were happy to have it off their hands."

Ty moved to take a closer look. It was excellent work, not that he was an expert on art. "Who painted it?"

Mandy tucked a stray lock of hair behind her ear. "No clue. It's not signed."

"Where would you even keep such a painting?" Tyler asked.

She snorted and waved her hand. "In the bedroom. From the discoloration on the wall when I went to assess the estate, Victor had it hanging at the head of his bed for years, decades probably."

What? That was completely fucked up. Ty glanced over at Craig and saw puzzlement on his face too. "Why would he do that?"

Mandy didn't understand his question. "I don't know, maybe he needed a little encouragement of the porn type? Maxwell is really put together."

"Oh for Christ's sake," Craig said. "Mandy, do you honestly think a full-size naked picture of an ex-boyfriend—looming over the bed of the man who probably murdered him—would in any way be conducive to getting it on with a new man?"

"Exactly," Ty agreed.

"What if Victor loved Maxwell?"

Ty grimaced. He'd loved Preston, or at least thought he could. "Did you say there was speculation of cheating? If that were a picture of Preston up there, the canvas would be hanging in shreds right about now."

Mandy's mouth rounded into a small O as she put the pieces together. "I guess I didn't think about it. I just thought, picture of naked man in gay man's bedroom, why not?"

Ty rolled his eyes and caught Craig doing the same thing. They grinned at each other. Craig understood. Ty was gay and Craig was straight, but they were both men. No way was a prospective partner going to be comfortable with such clear and obvious competition.

"Right, well, I haven't been out for a long time, but I've known I was gay since puberty. And I can tell you, I don't think most men would be different than women in this respect. Even if Victor had been in love with Maxwell... How would you have felt if the first time you went into Jake's bedroom, you were confronted with a life-sized nude picture of his ex-girlfriend?"

Mandy flushed and made a choking noise.

Now she got it. Ty gestured expansively at the painting. "This is not the same as pornography, let me assure you of that."

Craig nodded. "This convinces me that Victor did kill Maxwell."

Those words stabbed Ty in the heart. Maxwell would likely be dead of old age by now, but imagining the vibrant, beautiful, melancholy man murdered pained him.

"Why do you think that?" Mandy asked.

"Feels like a souvenir to me. Lots of killers keep something from their victims. Anyone want some more beer or water?" Craig asked.

"Sure, thanks. I'll take a beer," Ty replied while Mandy shook her head.

After Craig left the room, Mandy turned to Ty, her face pale and eyes stricken. "Tyler, I'm sorry. Maybe this wasn't such a good gift after all. I thought you'd be, I don't know, intrigued or something. But now it seems crass and gruesome."

He pulled his sister into a quick hug. "Don't be silly. I am intrigued. In fact, I think I might read up on the scandal."

"Oh, okay. Should we get Craig to hang it somewhere else?"

Ty sighed. When had Mandy got it in her head that he was completely incompetent? He was a history professor, but that didn't mean he couldn't hang his own damn paintings.

"No, I like it there. He's not my ex-boyfriend, and I didn't kill him. For me? In my room? This is life-sized porn, although I'm guessing if the 'rents should ever forgive me, this will ensure they'll stay out of my room."

Mandy snickered. "Yeah, I have to admit, irritating Mom and Dad had crossed my mind. They'll come around. You'll see." She patted his shoulder. Ty was less confident, and wasn't sure he'd forgive them even if they did come to accept him.

"Hey, I've got your beer out here," Craig called from the living room.

Ty and Mandy left the bedroom since it didn't seem as though Craig was coming back.

"What, afraid if we drink under the shadow of that enormous cock, you'll start getting ideas?" Ty waggled his brows at his best friend.

"Shut up." Craig tossed a couch cushion at Ty's head while holding out a freshly opened beer.

Ty threw the cushion back before he sat down on the couch. They talked about nothing of significance for a few minutes before Craig slapped his thighs.

"Okay. I gotta get home and have a shower. Ma will kill me if I'm late for dinner."

Ty half thought about inviting himself along, but he wouldn't be able to relax, knowing all his stuff was still in boxes.

"Make sure you eat something." Craig mothered him more than Mandy or his parents had ever done, but Ty couldn't say he disliked it.

"What if I want to sit here and drink all night?"

"Right, sure. Drink yourself into a stupor with all this unpacking? Not a fucking chance. You'll be up all night as it is." Craig stood, clapped his hand on Ty's shoulder, and held out his other hand to assist Mandy to her feet.

Ty thanked them both again, without the energy to even follow them to the door. As soon as it clicked shut, he surveyed the boxes littering his apartment. The disorganization disturbed him, but his joy at living in an apartment without any haunting reminders of Preston fucking him was more than worth the temporary chaos.

A bath, with its whirlpool action, would revitalize him enough to get a few more hours of work in; the sweat and grime and heat were making him lethargic and lazy. No matter what Craig said, he wasn't going to stay up all night. He wasn't that obsessive. Really.

Maxwell blinked, letting his eyes adjust to the light, as though waking up after a long sleep. Which he supposed was true. He was no longer in Victor's estate. Or at least, he wasn't in any of the rooms of the estate he was familiar with, the most hated of which had been Victor's bedroom. Aside from a bed too large for a single person and some furniture, a number of cardboard boxes decorated the room. Had the move prompted him to unwelcome wakefulness? He remembered a man's voice, sweet and compelling as gingerbread, and a woman's voice, brisk and efficient.

A shudder wracked his body. Not that anyone would see—they never did. And why would they, if the sensation was nothing more than a self-deceptive delusion his mind created?

Paintings were kept for hundreds of fucking years. Was he going to have to spend eons trapped like this, with his goddamned penis on display because Victor had been a spoiled brat who was fascinated by the occult? Somehow he'd thought when the old bastard—*das Schwein*—died, he'd die too. And if he hadn't seen Victor die with his own eyes, he wouldn't have believed it. Now he believed that as long as this cursed painting existed, he'd be trapped, watching, longing to have his body—his life—back. Or, perhaps, longing for death. The key to breaking the curse was...impossible for him.

An incredibly gorgeous man with his head tilted to the side walked into the room and stood in front of him—or his image, rather. Wet, dark hair framed the most beautiful male face he'd ever seen. A defined nose and sharp cheekbones drew attention to exotically shaped eyes made up of a compelling polychromatic of green and brown and gold. His skin was pale, but a hint of sun-kissed bronze indicated some time outdoors. Shorter than Max had been in life, but not by a lot. He was slender, toned, and only wearing a towel.

For the first time in decades, the stirrings of arousal whispered through Max. Yes, he'd been trapped in a painting portraying his full erection, but arousal was an emotional, visceral response as much as, if not more than, a physical one. He couldn't respond physically, but if he'd had his body still, his prick would have been twitching and plumping. Suddenly, he was deeply envious of this man's wife.

When Victor had fucked various men in front of him, Max hadn't been aroused or jealous. Resentment overrode most other emotions. But now his resentment had another root cause. He'd never be able to slide a fingertip down that damp, tight chest. Slip it under the edge of the towel. Flick the fabric loose and drop to his knees to worship the cock underneath. Given the rest of the man, he had no doubt the concealed prick would be worth his fealty.

"Maxwell Friedland," the man said to Max's image, shocking the hell out of him. Victor had been the only one to speak to the painting directly, and anyone who'd witnessed it had thought him crazy—verrückt, as his mother used to say. A scream yawed through his brain as he tried to respond. How did this gorgeous specimen of a man know his name?

Yes, I am Max. Who are you?

"I wonder what happened to you." The man stepped closer. Individual water droplets, magnifying his golden skin, were clearly visible now, and Max's metaphysical tongue itched, craving to lick them away. Remembered sensations of desire intensified. Max's heart felt as though it were throbbing in the area of his chest, keeping time with the throbbing of a phantom phallus that no one could see or touch.

"You are beautiful."

What? Had he heard correctly?

"Did you have hair that color? Or is it a trick of the artist? Could you truly be this buff, or is this the way you wanted to be portrayed?"

Oh heavens. He had heard correctly. If he could, he'd be dripping precum right about now. Even the thought of the man being married didn't dampen Max's bizarre mental arousal. Victor had claimed the world had changed, society was more accepting of men of their bent, but in Max's experience, men like them hid what they were. Some of his previous lovers had been married, and if circumstances hadn't been what they were, he would have married a woman eventually too, consigning himself to a near-celibate existence.

He'd hated the pretense, the lies, and the adultery, but they were a necessary evil. Max couldn't imagine a place where gay men didn't have to sneak around. A world where they could live and love openly. Judging this one for hiding his nature would be the height of hypocrisy.

That sparkling, flecked gaze dropped to Max's groin. The man lifted a hand as though he were going to touch.

Bitte...please...do it. Max was aware of a tactile sensation when someone touched his painting, like a soft breeze or a ghost walking through a room. Victor hadn't done it often, thank God, but Max found himself yearning to experience it again.

Max spied a bit of movement under the man's towel, followed by a blush and him lowering his hand.

"I can understand Victor keeping a painting of you in his bedroom. But I can't believe he would destroy such beauty. I can't believe he murdered you."

Nein. He didn't. Victor had done much worse than murder him. Max had screamed his throat raw—or tried to—every time a police officer came into Victor's room, but no one ever heard.

"I wonder how much Mandy paid for you. It's hard to believe such a gorgeous painting could be considered scandalous. Scandal seems old-fashioned, doesn't it?"

Says the gay man married to a woman. The man's cheeks were still rosy, and he flicked his gaze furtively around.

"Shit. I can't believe I'm talking to a painting. That's got to be an all-time low. Yet another thing to thank Preston for." A frown marred those perfect features.

Who was Preston? And why did Max want to punch him? Nevertheless, he wanted the pretty man to keep talking. He missed human interaction. Near the end of Victor's days, when there was no fucking but merely the indignities of the infirm, Victor had talked to him more and more. Max hadn't realized in the intervening...years...how much he appreciated that, even from a horny old goat like Victor.

Smooth shoulders shrugged, and Max couldn't help but follow the interplay of muscles rippling below the skin. He'd had sex a few times but never had the leisure or opportunity to admire his lovers even partially nude—the interactions were hurried, furtive. Victor had paraded naked men in front of him over the decades, but none he could pretend was his own, bared for Max's pleasure.

The man stepped closer still. If Max had all his senses, he'd be able to smell the scent of clean, musky male skin. Lips trembling, he wanted to kiss, lick, suck. If Victor knew of Max's torment, he'd be laughing himself sick in Hell.

"I don't know. There's something about you. You're the hottest man I've ever seen, but you're sad. Did you know, when this was painted, Victor was going to kill you? Shit. Mandy has to have more information. She had to know I wouldn't be able to stand not knowing."

Was Mandy the wife? Max didn't care about her; he wanted to know what this man's name was. Not knowing his name made it harder for Max to pretend he was at least a companion. The man strode out of the room, leaving Max with a sense of loss.

Mere moments later, the man returned, carrying a small, slim rectangular box. Settling down at the desk, he flipped open the box. The towel slipped precariously low, leaving Max with a tantalizing glimpse of a shadowed cleft between his buttocks.

As soon as Max saw the keyboard, he realized the box was nothing more than a "laptop" computer. Victor had had one in the latter days of his life, but nothing as sleek-looking. Either this beautiful, sexy man was wealthy, or technology had progressed beyond what Victor had had access to at the time of his death. Max sighed. Pornography. Through careful observation and lack of anything else to do, Max had determined computers were useful for easy typing and mathematical functions, but Victor used his for smut ninety-nine percent of the time. As much as Max hated him, there was something almost admirable about his single-mindedness, even after the flesh was no longer willing.

Where was the man's wife? Did she condone such behavior? Max hadn't spent time with many women besides his mother and sisters, but he couldn't imagine letting any wife know about such intensely arousing, yet abominably inappropriate, visuals.

"Maxwell Friedland. There's not a whole lot of information on you, is there?"

Max didn't know what the man meant, but didn't mind looking and listening. He didn't know why the man spoke to him directly, but it warmed him like nothing Victor had ever done. It didn't hurt that the man's voice ignited desire deep in the pit of Max's stomach.

A door slammed, and the towel-clad man jumped up. The towel slid to the floor and—dammit—he crouched and refastened it before Max got a look at more than his rounded, muscular bum.

A dark-haired woman burst into the room, but Max didn't care. His attention was on the half-naked man, and Max had already learned enough of his visual cues to know he was not happy.

"Mandy, what the fuck? How did you get in?"

Mandy shrugged. "I forgot my sunglasses."

"In my bedroom?" Outrage flavored the dulcet tones.

"No, of course not in your bedroom. I just popped in to say hi while I was here."

"But...but..."

Mandy's gaze flicked over to Max before landing on the open computer. "Oh my God. You weren't masturbating, were you? Tyler, you naughty, naughty boy."

Tyler! Finally Max could put a name to that gorgeous face, but the discussion of masturbating quickly drew his attention. He wasn't sure he'd ever seen anyone who wasn't a redhead blush so fiercely. Tyler had been doing no such thing, but Max hoped to witness it soon.

"No, of course not. But you can't just barge in. What if I had someone over?"

If she wasn't Tyler's wife, was she his girlfriend?

Mandy laughed, a short, mocking sound. "Yeah, right. You're not exactly a wild child, brother mine."

Brother. Tension flowed away. He shouldn't care, shouldn't be possessive of Tyler. Tyler would never know Max was here, watching.

"So? I could be." Only Tyler's back was visible, and his spine stiffened as he drew up to his full height.

As Mandy had said earlier, *Yeah, right.* Quite a novelty, in his experience—a man who didn't lie well. But it was a trait Max admired, though it must be difficult for Tyler to keep his sexuality a secret.

"You haven't made a lot of progress yet." Mandy waved her hands at the boxes stacked along the walls.

"Gee, thanks. Just what I needed—a critic."

"Hey, whoa. You're awfully cranky."

"Of course I am." Again Tyler sat in the chair by the desk. "I'm hanging around in a towel, and you waltz in without even knocking. I was looking forward to an evening by myself. How did you get in, anyway?" More lies. Somehow Max knew Tyler didn't want to be by himself, but Mandy wasn't the company he wanted.

"I'm sorry, Ty. Actually, your door was unlocked. Honestly, that was maybe okay at your old apartment, but I wouldn't do it here."

"Oh shit. No, you're right. I guess I just forgot. While you're here, I wanted to ask—do you have any more information about Maxwell?"

"Maxwell? Oh, the painting. I don't know; I haven't finished sorting and cataloging the estate. Why?"

"You got me interested earlier, but there's almost no information on the Web about him. I was curious."

Mandy shot her brother a skeptical look and shook her head. "I'll keep an eye out for anything and let you know. I'm guessing anything related to him will be a quick and cheap sale, as far as Victor's heirs are concerned."

A quick, cheap sale. Max grimaced. Victor would have considered it a fitting end to their association.

"Come this way." A faint hint of a British accent had colored the butler's words.

Max had never been to a house where he'd been greeted by a butler, never mind one imported from England. The clothes he'd worn were at least clean, but they were immeasurably shabby compared to the opulent home. But what else was he to do? He and most of the laboring population were barely surviving, and gaunt increasingly became the look du jour.

He hadn't considered supporting himself with his painting, but now he had no farm and no family to worry about. He had nothing but spare time, and the rich were the only ones with funds.

Apparently, being a butler paid rather well. The elderly man was dressed better than Max and didn't have that "I can only afford to eat once every other day" look the general populace had, Max included. "Mr. Cranston will be with you in a moment."

The man looked down his nose at Max before he slipped out of the room. Max glanced around. He hadn't been invited to sit, and quite frankly, he'd be uncomfortable doing so.

Without any clear indication of how long he'd be waiting for the man who'd offered to be his sponsor, Max settled for standing near the window and viewing the landscape. Cracking his knuckles, he tried to calm the flutters in his belly—Victor Cranston's correspondence had more or less promised Max a place.

For all of Victor's wealth, society took a dim view of someone who flaunted his proclivities as Victor did. Although it had been years since Max felt safe enough to indulge, he shared those same proclivities. Victor Cranston would hopefully make the perfect sponsor for him.

Movement at the door caught Max's eye.

"Good morning, Maxwell." Victor's gaze dropped down to Max's scuffed and almost-worn-through boots, traveled slowly upward past his threadbare, faded pants, and lingered, uncomfortably, at his groin before continuing back up to Max's face.

"Good morning, Herr Cranston." If Max had been wearing a cap, it would have been in his hands, and he'd have been wringing it. Subservience came easier the more desperate one was for food, and he'd already hit bottom. It couldn't get much worse, and Victor Cranston could be his ticket to...not wealth, but at least three square meals a day and a roof over his head. "It's a pleasure to finally meet you in person."

Victor's gaze dropped below Max's belt again as he spoke. "Call me Victor."

Huh. Max didn't enjoy this sensation at all. Victor was good-looking, yes. But he was young, maybe a decade younger than Max's thirty years. He felt a lot older than that these days. Hardship, death, and near starvation added weight to the soul and years to the shoulders. Unless something drastically changed in Victor's life, he'd never know the deprivation Max had experienced.

An air of entitlement wrapped around Victor like a cloak, and every word he spoke told Maxwell where he stood: beneath Victor's heel. Or perhaps at the end of his leash. Certainly, if Max had a choice, he'd have been standing anywhere but there. His options were limited, and maybe painting could help fill the void in his heart where his parents, sisters, and brother resided as ghosts.

"Stavers will show you to your room in the carriage house. There's a studio set up there, as well; you'll have to share it with Grant, a sculptor I'm also sponsoring."

"That's fine, Herr—I mean, Victor." Max had never had a conversation like this. After the initial glance, Victor hadn't raised his focus to Max's face once. Sheer force of will kept his hands relaxed at his sides instead of instinctively covering his privates. Surely Victor didn't expect any more of him than painting, did he? Under normal circumstances, Max might be amenable, but these circumstances were far from normal. And he suspected their sexual styles would be at complete odds.

"I'll expect to see you for drinks in the parlor this evening at eight."

"Yes, Victor. *Danke*."

The prospect of a hot meal set Max salivating. He could wait several more hours—it had been days since his last decent meal. Besides, he needed to return to his rooming house and pack up his meager belongings. He hadn't wanted to presume anything until Victor confirmed his status.

"You'll do perfectly," Victor said as he strode out of the room without so much as a by-your-leave.

Max stared after him. He couldn't afford the luxury of discomfort. Not now, not this close to regular meals he didn't have to scrounge for and a free place to sleep. He just hoped he was mistaken about the price Victor expected him to pay--

Tyler's return to the bedroom—alone—startled Max out of his reverie. It was almost like being wakened from a particularly vivid dream, and yet his incorporeal body required no sleep. He could only assume the "dreams" came when his attention drifted.

After making the bed, Tyler turned off the lights and lay down, towel still around his waist. A small amount of ambient light made his beautiful form visible as he stretched out on top of the covers.

Enticing movement underneath the towel from a twitching prick indicated he wasn't quite ready for sleep.

Sucking in a breath—and Max still didn't know why he did that since he no longer had lungs to breathe with—he waited with anticipation as Tyler lightly stroked his chest with one hand.

Tyler rolled a nipple between his fingers and pinched, letting out a gasp.

Fascinated, Max watched while Tyler gave his other nipple the same treatment. Tyler rubbed and pulled, and the towel around his hips drew up as the impressive erection underneath became more prominent.

Tiny thrusts of Tyler's hips shifted the towel just enough to give Max a hint of what hid beneath the fabric. A futile plea for Tyler to bare himself rose in Max's throat.

The sepia tones of the darkened room refused to reveal the flush of arousal on Tyler's skin, but his elevated breathing was audible. The anticipation was killing Max, and he couldn't believe how aroused the show made him, considering he was nothing more than canvas on the wall.

With a throaty groan, Tyler shoved his hand under the towel and grabbed his prick. The towel fell away, leaving Max with one of the most spectacular visuals he'd seen in a long time. Now he wanted Tyler to turn the lights back on, show him that honey-hued skin in its glorious nudity. He wanted to see how the flush of blood lengthening and hardening Tyler's shaft contrasted with the fist Tyler used to tug and stroke his erection.

The hand previously plucking at his nipples moved down to cup and roll his balls. Tyler's hips thrust off the bed, and he moaned. Max strained against his prison again, wanting to see, wanting to touch. All the invectives he'd hurled at Victor for placing him at the head of the bed, giving him a close view of Victor fucking every gold-digging nancy boy, came back to haunt him. Max wanted to be back at the head of the bed. This angle didn't let him properly see Tyler's expression. Didn't allow him to see Tyler's fingers wrapped around his sac.

Tyler drew up one leg and shifted a hand. Max whimpered. Tyler was diving for his puckered entrance, and Max couldn't see a damned thing! The leg, which Max would dearly love to have wrapped around his waist as he pushed his length into Tyler's hole, even now blocked all but the slick head of Tyler's prick.

Tyler growled, pulled his hands away from his genitals, and turned away from Max. Max gaped. *Nein*, he couldn't be done. He couldn't tease like that, could he?

Tyler! Max's shout was—as ever—in vain.

Tyler turned back, erection jutting from his hips. Max waited, hoping whatever Tyler planned next would give him a good view. If Max didn't know better, he'd think he was on the verge of coming. Ridiculous. He couldn't touch himself, mostly because he didn't have a body to touch. He'd never come without stimulation before, and he didn't think he was going to start now that the only cock he had was made of oil-based paint.

Tyler rose on his knees, back straight, and squeezed a small amount of lube into his palm. Max knew what it was, but he'd never touched any. He'd never had enough money to spend on such a luxury—even when he'd had the rare opportunity for more than a blowjob or handjob. The few times he'd fucked someone, spit had been the lubricant of choice, and he'd never fucked or been fucked by Victor. Thanks to Victor's continual taunts, Max had an encyclopedic knowledge of the different uses for lube, butt plugs, and countless other sexual toys he'd never be able to use. Max had only sketchy knowledge of current events, politics, and economics. And now, he didn't even know how many years it had been since Victor's death.

Did lube feel like cum? Or oil? Lotion, maybe? Of all the inventions Victor had paraded through his bedroom over the decades, lube was in the top three Max wished he had personal experience with.

Mein Gott. If Max's eyes could pop out, they would. Tyler spread his knees a little farther but remained upright. One hand, fingers shiny with lube, went between those firm, round cheeks. The other, with slickness coating the palm, moved to grasp his throbbing prick. A breathy, wailing moan drifted over to Max as both hands began moving.

Max pressed himself against the canvas, trying desperately to get closer, but it was as useless as ever. He kept his gaze glued to the action at Tyler's hips, and his own phantasmic hips mirrored Tyler's thrusts.

Rhythmic, guttural grunting accompanied Tyler's motions, and Max became aware of Tyler looking at him while he stroked off. Victor had done the same thing thousands of times, and it had disgusted Max every time. When Tyler did this, it was like a caress...no, firmer. Like Tyler was stroking Max off too.

Tyler's expression screwed up, and he took his gaze off Max to throw his head back. Max moaned as Tyler cried out and that gorgeous dick erupted, spewing thick white cum all over Tyler's hand and belly. Max wished he could smell it, the sharp, musky smell of male completion. Max inhaled, almost frantic, but that was yet another sensual dimension the curse denied him.

Tyler slumped, fingers slipping out of his ass.

What did he do now? Max was trapped on the burning brink of arousal, with no way to jump over into the oblivion of orgasm. Even as he reveled in the fact that Tyler could actually arouse him, he viciously cursed Victor for this agony.

Slowly, as his breathing returned to normal, Tyler unwrapped the hand holding his softening prick. He brought his fingers to his mouth and licked at the cum coating them.

Max screamed as he hurtled over an edge he didn't know he could traverse, and his world pulsed around him.

When Max could see past the crimson haze, Tyler was snuggled under the covers, a hint of a smile chasing the corners of his lips. As Tyler slid into slumber, Max's mind churned.

Was it possible to have a mental orgasm? There were no physical indicators, obviously, but the sensations of orgasm were as he remembered them. Nothing like this had ever happened since that awful, awful day Victor had captured him, punished him for refusing to let Victor fuck him.

How he wanted Tyler, wanted desperately to touch his skin, taste his body, immerse himself inside Tyler. Or even sleep beside his warm body. Max had never slept with anyone before. He settled back to watch over Tyler, enjoying the small miracle of pleasure he'd been granted.

Ty flipped back the covers and stood up. His gaze centered immediately on Maxwell's painting. Last night had been one of the best orgasms he'd had, by himself or with another, in a long time. Did it have anything to do with watching the spectacular hunk of man on display in his room? Perhaps. He wondered if he should feel embarrassed, but instead he had a new kinship for Maxwell. It hadn't been like getting off on porn; it had been intimate, like Ty had put on a show for a lover. Somehow that made it more exciting. Which was stupid. Masturbating for a painting like it was a lover was the kind of thing preceding a fairly serious break with reality.

"Good morning, Maxwell." Talking to the painting wasn't any better, but it wasn't easy to ignore Maxwell. So what if Ty got a little company from a painting? Might even be saner than talking to himself. As long as he didn't expect or imagine any responses, he could consider himself sane. Ignoring the painting hardly seemed polite or sensible, like ignoring the elephant in the room.

Glancing around, Ty was amazed he'd been able to sleep in the chaos of his new apartment, and slept late too. No matter what he'd said to Craig and Mandy, he'd expected to stay awake most of the night to unpack. But he'd been surprisingly horny, and he wasn't ready to become the fuck-'em-and-duck-'em guy he was planning on. After he'd come harder than ever, he'd wanted nothing more than to go to sleep, wishing Maxwell's hard body had been curled up around him.

"I should unpack more. This place is a disaster." Ty directed his words at Maxwell as he drew on a pair of sweatpants. "But I find it hard to believe there's so little information on you. This isn't exactly my area of expertise, but I can't believe I'm incapable of finding out what happened to you."

The more he spoke, the more...attentive... Maxwell seemed, as though listening in companionable silence. Maybe the breakup with Preston had sprained his sanity. No. Ty didn't believe that. If anything made him truly crazy, it would have been the cold and hurtful reception following his coming out to his parents.

"What do you think, Maxwell? Or can I call you Max? Max is a little easier to say. Hope you don't mind." Ty had almost called out the name as he'd come last night. Foolish.

Yep, he was certifiable. Regardless, yesterday's loneliness had diminished somewhat. He glanced at the boxes begging to be unpacked and his messenger bag bulging with papers to be graded, before sitting in front of his laptop defiantly. There were only a couple of days left on his mid-summer break, and he'd promised to attend a Canada Day celebration with Craig later today, but he could spare an hour or two for an extracurricular research project. He could put off unpacking for a while because he'd already unearthed the basics. Like lube. Ty coughed, glad he didn't need to justify that to anyone.

Stretching and feeling his spine pop made Ty feel each one of his twenty-nine years and then some. His biceps and quads burned too. Obviously moving was a lot more effort than a typical workout at the gym. Next time, he was hiring movers. Assuming he ever left this apartment—he was still enthralled by his good fortune.

Time to stretch his mental muscles instead. Tyler leaped into the virtual world of the Internet.

CHAPTER TWO

Ty rolled out of bed with a groan. How had he slept so damned long? Stretching, his joints snapped and crackled, an audible reminder that he'd made some poor choices this weekend. The move had been tough enough—he should have hired movers damn it—followed by an all-day barbecue to celebrate Canada Day at his friend, Josh's, place. If he hadn't taken that to mean all-day drink fest as well, he might have had a more productive Saturday, rather than spending the whole day in bed recuperating from a hangover the likes of which he hadn't had since he'd caught his boyfriend cheating and his parents had disowned him. Didn't help that approaching thirty meant he was no longer well-equipped to abuse his body in the same manner he did when he was a student at the university, rather than a professor.

At least the headache and the roiling nausea were gone, but he still wasn't sure if the muscle aches were the result of the move or dehydration from some ill-advised drinking while out in the sun.

After stumbling out of the bathroom, his loose sweat pants threatening to slip off his hips, the sight of Max in all his glory rocked him back on his heels.

"Oh. Max. Good morning." He glanced at the alarm clock on his bedside table. "Er, afternoon, rather." Three in the afternoon, and he had to be back at the university tomorrow. Despite his inclination to speak to Max as though he were a real person, it was a good thing he wasn't because Ty had not been at his most impressive since Max had showed up.

His stomach growled, protesting its hollowness. No wonder, really. Food hadn't been on yesterday's agenda, but he was starving now. He opened his laptop and ordered a pizza to be delivered. Craig would yell at him, but it was the easiest solution to his sudden and immediate hunger. In addition to the unpacking and grading he'd deftly ignored since Thursday, he'd managed to not buy any groceries either.

Out in the kitchen, he opened the fridge anyway. Still no food, and far too much beer left over from the move. No way was he drinking any more beer this weekend. Behind the half-empty case of beer, a few no-name caffeine-free, sugar-free cola cans lurked. He didn't know why his sister foisted that shit off on him when all she'd done was steal his beer anyway, but it was cold, wet, and not alcohol so it would have to do.

While he waited for his pizza, he half-heartedly unpacked a couple boxes of dishes. He needed to get this apartment in order, but since he'd more or less squandered his weekend, and he was behind on his marking, he was going to have to squeeze it in around other things. Not exactly like him. No matter how excited he was about living in such a great place, he couldn't muster up any enthusiasm for the drudge work of unpacking. Not when the siren call of finding out more about Max sang to him, luring him in. Then again, what most people mistook for fussiness was just a form of gentle obsession, and right now, having his belonging unpacked, his apartment organized, or being caught up on his grading weren't the obsessions most prominent in his head.

Thirty minutes later, he returned to his bedroom and plopped down in the oversized plush chair—as new as the couch—with pizza and a weird non-cola. This seat was better than the desk chair, as it gave him a clear sight line of Max. Ty would have to thank Mandy again. He'd never get tired of the view.

He picked up his messenger bag and sighed. There wasn't much chance of him making a dent in his grading, and he didn't think he'd be very forgiving of mistakes today. But he was well aware he was rationalizing a reason to ignore his responsibilities. Maybe he could allow himself an hour or two to fish for information on Max, but that was it. Then he'd have to do some real work.

Two hours passed by in the space of a heartbeat, much like every time Ty researched topics he was interested in, although he'd never cared to track down anything this recent before. He rolled his neck, stretching muscles too long held motionless aside from the click of keys.

He swallowed the last of his pseudo-cola and grimaced. Flat and warm made it taste even worse, if that was possible.

"Okay, Max, I've got a few places to start looking for you. Not everything is online, you know." Ty tilted his head. "Funny. I feel like I should explain that. After all, if the rumors are true, you didn't live to see computers, and the Internet was developed, like, fifty years after you died. Half of what I say would be a mystery to you."

Maybe talking to the painting like Max was in the room was completely mental, but he didn't care. He was more relaxed and more himself than he'd been in months. Actually it was kind of a cool role reversal for a history professor, lecturing a man from another time about the modern world. Imagining Max was real and listening to him was possibly the craziest thing he'd ever done, but he didn't care. Professors, especially history ones, were almost obliged to have eccentricities. Apparently, this was his, and it was harmless, although he wasn't really in a hurry to advertise it. Mostly because that would mean sharing Max and he wasn't willing to do that. Nevertheless, he gave Max a mini-history of the Internet. Lecturing was lecturing, and if he didn't like it, he probably would have hated his job.

He picked up a cold slice of pizza from the box, and around a mouthful of pizza, he expanded on what he'd discovered about Max.

"I'm going to have to dig into the county archives, but I think I've got a starting place. There was a lot more information on Victor, but surprisingly little from his early years. I even ordered an autobiography written by an artist who was involved in...well, I suppose it would be nice to call it a May-December romance, with Victor. I think there might have been a substantial financial incentive behind it, though. Anyway, this guy, Antoine LaRose, was Victor's lover in the eighties, when Antoine was apparently eighteen. Not like you would have known Antoine, but I'm hoping he might have something to say about you or your painting, because he's also a painter. We'll see."

He'd been so damn spoiled, and had gotten used to instantaneous delivery, but for this one the delivery time had been between six and eight weeks and he'd been aghast. The book had been published several years ago, and was technically out of print. It apparently hadn't been popular enough for the publisher to see fit to produce an ebook version, so Ty was stuck waiting for some book reseller to lay hands on it and ship it via the snailiest snail mail possible.

A muffled knocking interrupted Ty's monologue, and he got up to answer the door. Who knew he could carry on a one-sided conversation like this? If the painting were smaller, maybe it would be easier to ignore, but the sense that someone else—someone friendly—was in the room with him was unmistakable.

Max watched Tyler leave the room. He wanted Tyler to stay and talk some more. He was fucking lonely. Despite the people in Tyler's life, Tyler was either as lonely as Max or inherently chatty. Max didn't give a damn either way as long as the conversation continued.

Antoine. It had been years since Max had thought of Antoine, but Max remembered him—rather well, in fact. He'd stuck around the longest. Victor had thought it was because Antoine truly loved him. Max believed Antoine loved Victor's money more than any of the other boy toys Victor had and had been willing to put in a lot more time and effort to get it.

Like every other person Victor brought into his bedroom for the first time, be it a potential lover or servant, Antoine had given Max a noticeable double take. The servants usually followed up with a sign to ward off evil. Potential lovers split between anger and lustful appraisal. Antoine had been slightly different.

Although it seemed like Victor's boys were getting younger every year, in truth, it was Victor who was getting older. His boys were always between eighteen and twenty-four. Which was yet another reason for Max to despise Victor for doing this to him. When they'd met, Max hadn't fit Victor's typical profile, not even close. Victor had been twenty-two and Max eight years older. Over the decades, he had come to know Victor's type very well. And Max was not it. Max wasn't slender and breakable-looking. Max wasn't pale and bony. Max wasn't short and skinny. Victor never had any other type in his bed.

Antoine was the right age and physicality, but he was the most unusual man Max had seen up until then. He was the first of Victor's boys in the eighties and the first Max had seen with the wild, bleached blond hair sticking up in every direction. He was the first who'd regularly worn eyeliner and lip gloss. He was also the first Max had seen with body piercings and tattoos.

When Antoine walked into the room, Max's gaze had been drawn to him as quickly as Antoine turned his attention to Max's painting. Max hadn't been aroused, but he'd definitely been intrigued.

"Who's that?" Antoine jerked his head toward Max.

"Maxwell Friedland." Victor gave Max his customary smug, mocking smile. The one that said, "*How do you like being trapped in there while I'm out here? Because I fucking love it.*"

"You really have a painting of him?"

Victor raised a brow. "Of Max? Why wouldn't I?"

"Didn't you kill him in a jealous rage?" If Antoine truly thought that, Max didn't understand how he could have sex with Victor, never mind be excited by it. Who wanted to get involved with someone who might have killed their lover in a fit of madness?

"Don't be ridiculous, boy. Get on the bed and strip."

Those two sentences embodied everything Max despised about Victor. His entitlement, his assumption other people were playthings, his indifference to anyone else's feelings were the reasons Max had vowed he'd never succumb to Victor's invitation to bed. And he hadn't, but look where it had gotten him. Every one of Victor's boy toys had been cut loose within months—or in Antoine's case, two years—with some expensive parting gifts. Max didn't think his principles had been worth the price he'd paid to uphold them, but he'd never been good at faking things he didn't feel.

"In a minute. Was he your lover? Because that's a fucking awesome package there."

Wasn't the first time Max had heard that, or variations on that theme. Of course, he had no idea if the erection on display had any bearing on his true proportions, since he couldn't see or feel himself. For all Max knew, his penis represented some exaggerated fantasy of Victor's. The compliments might have been nice if they were commenting on his actual equipment. And assuming he had the intention or ability to ever use it again.

"No. He wanted to be, but he left before we could get it on."

What? That good-for-nothing fraud.

Antoine nodded and moved closer, inspecting every inch. "It's good." This time Max knew he wasn't talking about Max's dick, but the quality of the painting. Like everything else, though, Victor had cheated on that too.

"Who painted it?"

"I did."

Lies. Victor was responsible for this travesty, but he sure as shit hadn't painted it. Max often wondered if the pendant responsible for his predicament was visible around his neck. The chill of the carved stone pendant against his throat was the last true physical sensation he'd experienced.

"You did?" Antoine didn't bother to hide the incredulity in his voice as he whipped around to stare at Victor, who was already more than half undressed, erection poking up over the waistband of his underpants. He kept in shape, but he was not the same man who'd tried to coerce Max into having sex all those years ago.

"Greatest *trompe l'oeil* in the world."

Trick of the eye. Yes, he was. Victor was such an asshole. But Antoine's immediate recognition of the word confirmed he had a passing familiarity with art terminology.

"You're kidding. I don't see it." Antoine stepped closer, his expression more clinical now. "Tell me. What's the trick?"

Victor glared at Max.

If Max could, he would have told Antoine that to keep Victor's interest, he'd have to display less interest in anything or anyone else. The exasperated huffing and contemptuous glares were excellent indicators of Victor's impatience. He gestured at the bed.

"Hurry up, already." Ah, Victor and his unattractive, unromantic "I deserve your subservience" sexual style.

"It looks perfect. Why haven't I heard more about your work?" Antoine began to strip mechanically, more interested in the conversation than the sex. For which Max didn't blame him one bit, but Victor would not agree.

"I only had the one masterpiece in me. I prefer to foster others' talent. Talent like yours." Victor stroked Antoine's half-hard dick while Max wondered if this was yet another double entendre.

The talent Victor wanted to foster was more in Antoine's pants than anywhere else. As the years went by, the artistic capabilities of Victor's lovers decreased as his desperation to fuck nubile young men increased. In fact, Antoine's artistic tendencies surprised Max. He'd thought Victor had given up on the delusion of being an art sponsor.

As soon as Antoine was naked, Victor smacked him on the butt. "Get on the bed and suck me." Antoine did as he was told, on hands and knees to reach Victor's prick. From Max's vantage point, Antoine did appear to have skills, even if they weren't art related. A beautiful depiction of a dragon graced Antoine's slender back, tail caressing one rounded butt cheek before wrapping around a thin but well-formed thigh.

Tattoos as art were a revelation for Max, but Antoine's couldn't be called anything else. If the boy had been in Max's bed, well, he would have wanted to trace every inch of the colorful ink with his tongue, maybe trail his prick, slick with precum, along the path of the Prussian blue tail.

Antoine used one hand to anchor himself and another to caress Victor's balls. When he moaned around his mouthful, Victor flashed a triumphant look at Max. Max laughed bitterly in his prison, Victor unable to hear his mirth, because Antoine still hadn't gotten hard.

After a few more minutes, Victor pulled away. "Enough, boy. Middle of the bed now."

Antoine faced Max on his knees, legs spread, blue eyes bright against the dark eyeliner. Max hadn't expected to, but he found Antoine attractive. Silver-colored hoops piercing both small nipples held Max's attention. He'd never seen nipple piercings before. If he hadn't been stuck in this painting, he might have tried to get Antoine into bed.

Victor smoothed a condom on before he clambered onto the bed behind Antoine. Lube squelched from a container, and from the grimace on Antoine's face, Victor hadn't applied any finesse with it.

"Hope you're ready, boy." There wasn't a chance for Antoine to reply before his body shook with the force of Victor's entry. After a few thrusts, the pinch of pain eased from Antoine's face. He began to tweak his nipples with one hand while jacking his dick with the other, all the while staring at Max's painted erection. When his gaze flickered up, a devilish grin on his face, Max knew the pulsing, ruddy erection rising from Antoine's body had very little to do with the man fucking him.

Antoine moaned again.

"That's it, boy. You like that? You like me fucking your ass?" Victor's thrusts became more vigorous.

"Oh, yes, I love it." Antoine's hand stroked faster. He licked his lips, his eyes fully focused back on Max's dick.

Victor groaned and shuddered behind him. Antoine never took his gaze off Max; only a couple strokes later, Antoine shot white streaks of cum over the bed. Victor pulled out and flopped on his back almost before Antoine's dick had stopped jerking.

Peering at the mess Antoine had made, Victor let out a self-satisfied grunt. "That was a good one, boy. Guess you'll be back for more."

"Guess I will," Antoine purred. He tapped Victor gently on the lips with his clean hand before he went in search of a cloth to wipe up with.

Max's incipient stirrings of arousal faded. Victor had used Antoine, as he did all of his disposable boys, but Antoine had used Max just the same, to convince Victor that Antoine was hot for him. Damn. If Max had a body, his skin would be crawling. He'd hated it when Victor treated him like a sex object, and Antoine had done the exact same thing, but it was a hundred times worse.

"I'll call you later." Victor slapped Antoine's ass. The young man quickly pulled on his clothes, glanced at Max once more, and left.

"What do you think of this one, Maxwell? He's sweet and pretty, isn't he? I know you're wondering if he's the one. Could you love him? Could he love you? I think, though, that he loves me. Much easier to love a warm body." Victor chuckled, the sound smug and self-satisfied.

Whenever Victor brought home someone new, he dangled the same old moldy carrot under Max's nose. If, by some astronomical long shot Max fell in love, how the hell would anyone fall in love with him? Apparently Victor had it on good authority that love would break the curse. Like it wasn't dumb fucking luck Victor had managed to trap Max with a curse he'd never believe in if it hadn't happened to him.

Antoine wasn't the answer to Max's situation. No one Victor brought home would be; he'd bet Victor's fortune on it.

Every time Victor had fucked Antoine over the next two years, Antoine had made sure he was facing Max, jacking off to Max, and Victor had smirked at him as he smoothed a hand over Antoine's rump. Max had felt like they were involved in some illicit three-way affair. The memory sickened him. Both of them had sickened him. But the disdain and disgust hadn't spilled over to a dislike of the piercings and tattoos. If he ever escaped this hell, he'd have to get some for himself, because he wasn't having sex again, which ruled out playing with them on another man.

Ty trailed Craig through the apartment to the kitchen, where he deposited a large sack in the fridge. Now that he lived closer to Craig, he wondered if these unannounced visits were going to become the norm.

"Thank your mom for me." Ty's stomach rumbled a little as he imagined what Mama D'Amato had packed for him. Then again, if Craig always brought his mom's leftovers as a peace offering, it was going to be difficult to be annoyed. At least Ty hadn't been jerking off.

"Sure thing. But start thinking about a Sunday that'll be good for you to come over for dinner."

"Why?"

Craig flipped open a couple cupboard doors and frowned. "I don't know. She said she wanted to have a little celebration."

Ty didn't need or get specific invitations. He was always welcome to accompany Craig when he went to a family event, but ever since he'd come out—and effectively lost his parents over it—Mama had been even more mothering than usual. "Okay, I'll be there. Same time as usual?"

"I guess. I'll let you know if it's different."

Craig grabbed a bottle of water out of the fridge and turned to survey the still-disastrous display of boxes. "I'm amazed. I thought all of this would have been unpacked already. But you got the bedroom set up already, right?" Craig didn't wait for an answer before he walked into Ty's bedroom. "Shit. Forgot about that."

Ty sprinted after him. "Forgot about what?"

Grimacing, Craig gestured at Max. "Him. In all his glory."

"Oh, right. Bet that gave you a shock." Ty laughed but stopped as soon as Craig eyed the pizza box by his desk and gave him a worried look.

"You had pizza last night?" His friend turned into a cop right before his eyes. Not that he wasn't a bit of a cop all the time, but Craig hadn't gone into work mode until he inspected the state of the bedroom.

"No, I had pizza for lunch." Ty certainly wasn't going to admit he'd been too hungover and/or dehydrated to eat much of anything for dinner.

Craig gave him a pitying look. "And you didn't unpack a single thing. Don't think I didn't notice the television and cable aren't hooked up. Are you okay? Did you hurt yourself?"

Ty huffed. No one thought he could take care of himself. "I'm fine. I'm just trying not to overdo it."

Craig peered at him, and a twinge of sympathy for every criminal Craig had interrogated over the years made itself known. The quizzical, disbelieving stare was intimidating, almost compelling him to confess every sin he'd committed. Good thing Craig had had to leave the barbecue early to head into work—Craig often had to work holidays—and hadn't been witness to just how much Ty had foolishly drank.

"Are you sure you're okay? What did you do last night?"

Right. That was enough. Craig was a good friend, but Ty wasn't that predictable, was he? If he was, he'd have to think about...not changing, but modifying his behavior. Throw out a surprise every now and then.

Craig was waiting for an answer. Ty wasn't obliged to satisfy Craig's curiosity, but maybe if he did, Craig would stop hounding him. "If you must know, I looked up some stuff about the painting. Then I jacked off and went to sleep." Only a slight modification of the truth.

Craig's face reddened instantly, and Ty stifled a giggle. He wasn't usually so blunt, but Craig—like Mandy on Thursday—was treating him like a child, and it had to stop. Maybe speaking his mind would be enough of a change.

"Tyler! What the fuck? Why did you tell me that?" Craig's gaze flickered over to Max's image, and his face flared hotter.

"Dunno. But you were acting like, I don't know...I'm incompetent or something." He certainly wasn't going to confirm Craig's obvious conclusion that Ty had been beating off over Max's image. Far too much information to share with his very straight friend—or anyone, really.

"Did I? I didn't mean to do that. I've been worried about you. Ever since you broke up with Preston, you've been a little erratic and a lot less...sure of yourself, I guess. When you wear sweatpants all day, don't leave the house, and generally act out of character, I get worried."

Oh. Craig wanted him back in his predictable rut. Breaking up with Preston had ultimately shifted the direction of his life. There were bound to be a few unexpected turns along the way, and Craig would soon adapt. Ty patted Craig's arm and smiled. He was lucky he had a caring, supportive friend. His other friends were supportive too, but Craig was like a brother to him. "I appreciate it. I do. But I've gone through some bad shit, and I wanted to take a break this weekend. I've got classes starting up again Monday." Working the summer session sucked the big one, but he'd hoped it would help keep him from thinking about his unwelcome single state.

"Fine, I'm sorry. But no more pizza this week, hear me? If you think about ordering any more, you call me. We'll go out or go to Mama's. If you need company or anything, call me. I'll even help unpack." Craig grimaced, and Ty almost laughed. He wouldn't inflict his persnickety organization on his much more laid back friend.

Tyler refrained from rolling his eyes. Craig had learned how to mother him from the best. But he was twenty-nine years old. He could eat pizza all week if he wanted to. With Mama D'Amato's leftovers in the fridge, it wasn't damn likely, but pizza was easy. Craig acted like he was ready to throw himself off a bridge. Which wasn't the case and never had been.

He'd been angry, hurt, and embarrassed over his breakup. Preston's infidelity had been a giant, flashing billboard proclaiming he wasn't in the relationship he wanted. When his parents had been unable to accept his sexual orientation, he'd been disappointed and hurt. But he wasn't depressed. Not really. The hurt Preston inflicted had long since faded, but he suspected getting used to being disowned would take more than six months, and as a result he was having difficulty being as social as he used to be. Pretending to be good company was a challenge, even to seek out no-strings sex.

Craig's face lit up. "What about going to a club on the weekend? I bet your clubbing buddies miss you, since they couldn't get off work to help you move."

Ty sighed. Going out to a club wasn't a bad idea. "I'll think about it. The move has put me a little behind with work, though. But if you really want to help..."

Craig peered around like he was ready to start opening boxes immediately.

Tyler grabbed his arm. "No, I don't mean around here. Do you have access to the police archives?"

"Yeah, sure." Craig's arm tensed under his fingers. Silly man. He should know better. Ty wasn't a troublemaker and wouldn't need anything from Craig that would get him in trouble.

"Can you get me the police reports on Max?"

"Max? Who is Max?"

This time Ty did roll his eyes, then gestured over Craig's shoulder. "Maxwell Friedland. The guy in the painting, remember?"

Craig relaxed. "Couldn't resist the mystery, eh? No problem, I can try to look into the old case files, see if I can get copies, if they still exist. What year, do you think?"

Tyler had done enough online research to know that, although he'd yet to delve into some of his other resources. "1937. He was reported missing by another artist in November."

"You don't know what day in November?"

"The source I found said the sixth, but I haven't found verification yet."

Craig pulled out his official notepad. He scratched out the particulars before returning it to his pocket. "I'll get to it when I can. With Jake out on leave, things are a little busier than normal."

Tyler smiled and hugged his friend. There was no hesitation in Craig's return hug. "Thanks. I appreciate it."

"Don't forget what I said about the pizza." Craig's expression was stern and authoritative. Ty almost had to take him seriously, even though he'd witnessed the milk from the nose incident when they were ten. "Mama would never forgive me if I let you eat crap all week, capisce?"

"Yes, officer, sir," Ty gently mocked him.

"That's Detective Sir," Craig teased back. "Okay, gotta go. Lock the door after me."

What was it about him that made people think he was so damn helpless? Nevertheless, he followed Craig and locked the door behind him. He warmed up a plate of leftovers before returning to his bedroom.

"That was my friend, Craig. Good-looking, isn't he?"

Yes, but not as good-looking as you. Jealousy was an emotion Max didn't recall, though he'd had no trouble recognizing it when Tyler had hugged the attractive, dark-haired man. But with Craig gone, Tyler talked as he ate, soothing Max.

"He's a great guy, and he's a detective on the police force. Between the two of us, I'm hoping we can figure out what happened to you. Not that it matters much now, but I'd be happier knowing you lived until old age, rather than been killed and hung as a trophy on Victor Cranston's bedroom wall, you know?"

Too bad all the detective work in the world wouldn't help Tyler. Even if by some weird twist of fate he figured out about the curse, there wasn't any way he could break it.

A piece of tomato dropped from Tyler's fork, splattering sauce on his naked chest before falling to the floor. "Oh shit."

Tyler plucked the tomato from the floor and tossed it into the garbage. He used his thumb to scoop up the sauce on his smooth chest and stuck it in his mouth.

Max whimpered. How could this be happening? Tyler was the sexiest man he'd ever seen, and he couldn't touch him or talk to him. Wasn't being stuck in this painting misery enough?

Plate in hand, Tyler left the room, Max watching the strong, bare back as long as it was visible. Before Max had a chance to miss him too much, he returned, empty-handed.

"I can't wait to look at those police reports." Tyler cast a longing glance at his computer. "As much as I'd like to get into the newspapers, I should grade at least a couple of those essays."

Newspapers? From eighty years ago? *Mein Gott*, they'd be in tatters. Did they even keep newspapers that long? Max didn't imagine a nobody like him had had much in the way of newspaper coverage. If Victor had been missing, that would be a different story. A big story.

Looking for all the world like a child denied a sweet, Tyler sat back at his desk and pulled a stack of papers out of his messenger bag. Even if Ty grading essays meant the end of his conversation with Max, it wasn't all bad. Max was content with the sense of companionship he'd not experienced since long before his entrapment.

CHAPTER THREE

Tyler slung his messenger bag on his desk, rousing Max from his semi-somnolent state. Max couldn't exactly call it sleep, but early on, boredom had necessitated him developing a sort of fugue state he could exist in when there wasn't anyone or anything to observe. Probably preserved his sanity, although until recently, Max hadn't been sure sanity was a beneficial commodity.

"Hey Max." Tyler wiped at his shiny forehead. "It's damn hot out there. Stinky humid, too. That's probably the worst part of teaching the summer session. Most of the buildings are too old for central air conditioning." He plucked at his short-sleeved pale rose button up shirt. Combined with the casual slate grey pants, he didn't much look like any professor Max had learned from.

Obviously, when Max attended university, professors dressed much more formally, but with the amount of television Max had watched with Victor, he'd had plenty of time to get used to more casual clothing. All of Max's professors had been stodgy old men or the occasional woman. None of Max's professors were as attractive and vibrant as Tyler.

"Now I definitely need to do some unpacking. Can't put it off forever. Besides, I managed to get caught up today on the grading I put off while I was packing and moving."

Tyler scrunched up his face. "Now, I just have to get caught up on the stuff I fell behind on while catching up from the move." He laughed, a musical sound Max wished he heard more of. "I guess that doesn't make much sense."

Snatching a navy garment out of one of his drawers, Tyler disappeared into the bathroom. A few minutes later, he returned wearing yet another pair of shapeless sweat pants, the kind Craig spoke of with such distaste.

The garment itself wasn't flattering, but they had a tendency to slip lower and lower on Tyler's slim hips and a couple of times, Max even saw the shadow of pubic hair.

There would be no crying from this painted man if those pants were to slide right off, give Max a full view in daylight of the prick that had engrossed him almost every night since Tyler had acquired him. Much to Max's chagrin, Tyler almost never stripped down in the bedroom, and Max had to rely on what he was able to see when Tyler masturbated at night, with the lights out. For the first time, Max became a willing and eager voyeur.

Tyler pulled a shapeless shirt from a pile of laundry and put it on. Max wanted to beg him not to, not the least of which was that Max wouldn't see anything at all if Tyler's pants fell off.

In lieu of a strip show, Max was content to observe the neat precision with which Tyler unpacked and placed his things. Several of them were accompanied by a story of how he got them. The smiles, the occasional snorts of laughter—Max loved it. Tyler was so uncomplicated, so genuine compared to Victor and the bottom-feeders he'd brought to his bed.

Tyler worked hard, nonstop for hours, sweat making the shirt cling to his chest. Shadows had lengthened substantially in the room when he came to a box of pictures and his previous animation fell away. He withdrew a wooden frame, gripped tightly in both hands.

Tyler raised his head, and if Max had truly been standing there, Tyler would have been looking him in the face. Who was in that picture? Why was Tyler upset?

"I could have sworn I'd ditched this." He placed the frame face down on his desk and shoved the box aside. "You know, I think I've unpacked enough for today."

When he returned, he carried an ice cream container and a spoon, and slumped in the plush chair by the bookshelf that looked comfortable but Tyler rarely seemed to use since he worked almost non-stop while in Max's visual range.

"I caught my boyfriend cheating on me at the faculty Christmas party. With my teaching assistant. I told you I was a history professor, right? Medieval Europe."

The pride in Tyler's voice as he spoke of his profession made Max smile almost as much as the increased naturalness of Tyler's conversations. As days bled into weeks, he treated Max more and more as though he were Tyler's companion in the room, rather than a sounding board on the wall. Even if Tyler hadn't specifically mentioned his profession, it hadn't been hard to figure out, not when Tyler graded papers over the past couple of weeks, complaining about a number of hilarious errors his students had incorporated into their essays. But your boyfriend cheating with your employee? That had to be awful, especially if you cared about the man. Some of Victor's squeezes had fucked the staff, with Max as witness, but Victor didn't care about any of them. And he never had the illusion or expectation of faithfulness that Tyler did.

"It was awful. We were at the faculty Christmas party for the history department. Preston had been distant all night..."

"Where'd your boyfriend go?" Wendy, one of his fellow professors, returned to the table with a glass of wine for each of them.

"Bathroom, I think." Ty didn't know for sure, but he'd brought Preston to enough social events over the past year they'd been dating that he knew a number of faculty members. It wasn't like he'd have no one to talk to. Besides, the past few weeks had been rather stressful, what with Ty spending a large amount of time grading papers and Preston dealing with clients who wanted investments in place before the end of the calendar year. Preston had been a little snippy in the car, and Ty would rather not fight. Not when there was a chance they'd have sex. It had been almost three weeks now, and Ty was damn horny.

"You and the kids going back west for Christmas?" he asked. Most of Wendy's family lived in Vancouver, a great place to spend the holidays—warmer with much less snow, although her ex and his family lived locally.

"Nah, not this year. It's easier for me and Bill to share the kids if I stay in town." The irritating drone of Preston's phone on vibrate interrupted her. Ty didn't recognize the number, but Preston's clients rarely allowed him a night to himself. His boyfriend was paranoid about the phone; Ty was amazed he'd left it on the table at all.

"Sorry, Wendy. I'd better go find Preston. I don't know how important this call is."

Wendy sniffed and waved him away. Ty had the same reaction to Preston's phone some days too. It interfered during both dates and sex, but Preston was an important man at his company, and Ty had learned early on the phone was like another of Preston's appendages.

Ty glanced around but didn't see Preston anywhere. Although their group wasn't confined to this room, he figured the next place to check would be the bathroom. On the way there, he thought he heard Preston's voice coming from the small classroom doubling as the coat check.

After weaving his way through the coat racks, he came to a halt, stunned. Preston had Ty's teaching assistant pressed face-first against the wall, trousers down around his thighs as Preston pounded into his ass. Ty was more than familiar with Preston's litany of raunchy sex talk, but he could have gone his entire lifetime without hearing Jeffrey's satisfied moans or his exhortations for Ty's boyfriend to fuck harder. Ty wasn't sure if he wanted to scream or throw up. In the end, he did neither.

Instead, phone clenched in his fist, he crept away and fled to an upstairs bathroom. He locked the door and closed himself in a stall, then sank down on the seat. With shaking fingers, he did something he'd never done before—he unlocked Preston's phone and snooped. The urge to throw up returned. The phone was filled with poison. Three different hook up apps with recent activity. Dick pics by the dozens, and most of them weren't actually Preston's. Texts and e-mails to several different men. Arrangements to meet and graphic descriptions of what would happen when they did. Many of the men Ty knew or had met. Far fewer work calls than Ty, as gullible as he was, had been led to believe. Relief loosened some of the tightness in his chest when he confirmed none of his close friends were on Preston's contact list. But the number of fuck buddies his boyfriend had was almost pathological. Including his dentist, for Christ's sake. Teaching assistants were littered all over campus. But dentists... Did Preston know how hard it was to find a good dentist? Asshole.

Thank all that was holy they'd never gotten to the point of going bareback, but Ty would still need to get tested. This level of deception made his heart clench and blood pound in his temples.

Ty stood and turned, holding his hand over the toilet. It would serve Preston right if he flushed the phone away, ruined the fancy new toy he'd waited in line for with hundreds of other spoiled brats who needed the next greatest gadget. He remained poised like that for several minutes, before realizing if he trashed the phone, he'd have to talk to Preston in person to break up with him—which decided it for him.

Heaving in a deep breath filled with the chemical scent of industrial deodorizers, he slipped the phone into his pocket and left the stall. He splashed water on his face at the sink, but he didn't know when the two bright spots of color on his cheeks and the wild look in his eyes would go away. Didn't matter. He had to quickly return the phone to the table and escape before he ran into Preston.

When he got downstairs, he saw his table through the crowd. Jeffrey and Preston were talking and laughing with Wendy, both looking innocent, although Jeffrey's hair hadn't completely escaped the aftermath of clandestine sex in the coat closet. Preston's hair and suit were perfect—apparently practice helped with that too.

No way could he do fake nonchalance. Heat simmered in Ty's face. If he spoke to Preston now, the confrontation would be humiliating and loud; he'd be gossip fodder for months, and Ty wouldn't put it past Dr. Carscadden, the head of the department, to remember this when he was up for tenure in a couple of years. Instead, he pulled out his own phone and texted Wendy—being as cryptic as possible—and ducked out of sight.

Within minutes, Wendy stood in front of him.

"What the hell is going on? What's wrong? Are you sick?" Wendy peered at his face. Ty let out a bark of bitter laughter.

"I just saw Preston and Jeffrey fucking." Ty was amazed he could say it aloud without hitting something.

"What? When?"

"Just a few minutes ago. In the coat room."

"You did not!" Wendy turned her head back toward the ballroom, although Ty knew she couldn't see Preston from here. "Wait, they did come back to the table together."

"Yeah, well, I was going to flush his phone, but instead I'd like you to slip it back on the table, if you could."

"Why? I say flush it. What an asshole. Er...I guess they're both assholes."

"Nope. I can't talk to him, Wendy. I just can't. This is the easiest way to break up."

"Oh, Tyler, honey. I'm sorry. I can't believe they'd do this to you. Are you sure about what you saw?"

Ty's laughter leaked out with a hysterical tinge. "Uh, yes. Even if I wasn't, he's fucking about four or five other guys on the side." Ty brandished the phone at her as her eyes widened.

"Slip it back on the table? Are you sure? I could cram it down his throat. And I never liked that Jeffrey. Always talks to the other TAs like they're his personal photocopy slaves." Wendy narrowed her eyes.

Ty's grin was likely more homicidal than happy. Wendy had his back. "No, thanks. Just get this back on the table. Don't say anything to them, please. I'm going to leave now, try to wrap my head around this." Figure out the best way to craft a break up text.

Wendy gave him a hug. Ty avoided the coat room entirely, ditching his cheap coat—it wasn't that cold out anyway. Quickly, he slipped out into the winter night and grabbed a cab.

Safely on his way home, he pulled out his own phone and sent a short breakup text.

Ty sighed and picked up the wooden frame. The first New Year's Eve they'd spent together. They'd been dating two months, having met at a Halloween party. He turned it to show Max, even though he hardly knew why he bothered.

"We looked happy, didn't we? You know, most people cheat when their relationship becomes unhappy. Funnily enough, I don't think Preston was ever unhappy. Just completely unwilling to be monogamous and truthful. Who knows? Maybe the sneaking about turned him on or something.

With a negligent toss, the picture landed in the trash can by his desk, the tinkle of broken glass unmistakable.

"I swear, Max, we were dating a year. I thought we were heading towards moving in together, taking the next step. I'm not sure he was faithful for even a solid week of our relationship. Bastard."

Ty fancied he saw sympathy on Max's face, undoubtedly his overactive imagination at work.

"He tried apologizing. Like I'd be stupid enough to take his cheating ass back. I didn't even mention catching him with Jeffery, not when I had all that ammunition from his phone. After all, I had to work another four months with Jeffrey until the spring semester was over. It was almost unbearable, especially listening to Jeffrey's fake condolences on my break up. Fortunately, I've got a new TA for the summer. Her name is Allison, and she's been great. And if the fates work in my favor, I'll be keeping her for the fall and winter, too."

Only another few days before he'd find out for sure, and then he could breathe easy. He stared into his Rocky Road. He'd wanted to drown his sorrows, but the memory of his last hangover was far too recent. Ice cream wasn't a bad substitute, but he should probably stop wallowing. Better to be out of a crap relationship than still in it, playing the fool. And it hadn't taken long before he figured out he'd never really loved Preston, but he'd certainly been in love with the idea of happily ever after.

"Guess I'd better take out the trash." Ty sneered at the wastebasket. "Then do some more work. I tell you, Max, it was all for the best. Despite Preston's douche-baggery, he made me realize when I was ready to settle down again, it would be with someone who'd be faithful. Someone I could love and someone who could love me. One day, I'll find that."

Ty looked up when his teaching assistant for the summer session poked her head into his office.

"I emailed you the links and login information for those newspaper archives you asked for."

He breathed a sigh of relief. "Thanks, Allison. I really appreciate it. You can take off now, if you'd like. I've only got another hour of office hours before I'm heading out."

"Thanks Dr. Williams."

One day, he'd get her to call him Ty. Other professors might prefer the formality, but Ty wasn't that far from being an eager TA, and the formality made him cringe. But there would be plenty of time to work on that, assuming he got his first choice of TA for the coming school year.

"May I ask why you're interested in those newspapers? They're a little out of your interest, aren't they?"

Then again, he didn't suppose Allison would have questioned anything he did at the beginning of the term, so maybe she was getting used to his style.

"Not hardly. I'm pretty sure trying to navigate newspaper archives, and especially microfiche, went a long way to deciding me on more ancient history."

Allison laughed. "With most newspapers putting their back issues online, it's a lot better than microfiche, but still a bit of a headache."

Ty wasn't sure he wanted to tell Allison the truth. He suspected his interest wasn't quite logical and he didn't want to defend his little project to all and sundry.

"Anyway, it's just a bit of research for my sister. She's brokering the sale of the Cranston estate and I'm just getting her a bit of history on some of the items."

Allison frowned, and for a brief moment Ty wondered if he was going to get a lecture on using university resources for personal purposes, even though it shouldn't be an issue as long as it didn't interfere with his normal duties.

"I thought your sister owned that store, Something Old. Isn't..." Allison's frown deepened. "I don't want to be insulting or anything, because Something Old is one of my favorite stores in the city—always something weird and wonderful there, sort of antiques, but not exactly high-brow, you know. Affordable for us working folks. And I'd have thought Victor Cranston would have a lot of very expensive art and maybe even antiquities."

"Mandy also owns another place in Hazelton Lanes where she auctions off the expensive stuff on behalf of the families, taking a cut of the final sale price. My sister isn't stupid, and she figured out a long time ago that it was easier to convince people to allow her to broker the auction if she also took the rest of the estate as one lot. Most people with relatives' estates to unload were happier with one-stop shopping as long as they were still getting top dollar for the expensive art and antiques. But that meant she was often left with a lot of things that didn't exactly fit in with her flagship store. She opened Something Old to sell the extraneous items. Although it's certainly not her primary area of interest, I know she's pleased with how successful it ended up being."

"Wow, that's really cool. Guess I'll have to go back in a few weeks, see what might have gotten in there from old Victor's estate."

Ty grinned. "Better give it a month. I have it on good authority that there was a lot of shi... I mean, a lot of stuff that needed to be cataloged and sorted."

"Inside scoop. Even better." Allison drew in a breath. "Well, I have to pick up a couple of books at the library then I'll head out. See you tomorrow, Dr. Williams."

"Bye Allison." Ty reluctantly returned his attention to the grading that he was still behind on, although slightly less so every day. With the summer session being so compressed, it was difficult to catch up. As anxious as Ty was to get into the newspaper archives, he didn't want to get sucked into personal research while at the office.

The halls were quiet, and Ty truly didn't expect any students. Any students with any sense were out in the sunshine—his last office hour of the day only got busy when there was a test or essay due the following day. He started packing up his things fifteen minutes early. No one was going to notice if he escaped now.

As he fastened the flap of his messenger bag shut, his office door slammed open and he straightened in alarm.

"What the fuck, Ty." Jeffery looked like a blond avenging angel, and for the first time, Ty became aware of their dissimilar builds. Jeffery might be a few inches shorter but he had a good twenty or thirty pounds more muscle. It had never occurred to him to fear Jeffery—they were academics—but a frisson of unease sparked to life in his belly.

But, he'd decided on a course and he was going to see it through, no matter how uneasy confrontation made him. Surely Jeffery wouldn't do anything stupid. Or at least, nothing stupider than fucking his supervisor's boyfriend at the Christmas party. He did rather regret Jeffery had taken to addressing him as Ty, though. In this situation, he wouldn't have minded a little more formality.

"Good afternoon, Jeffery. Are you enjoying your summer?" The one thing that had saved his sanity had been the fact that Jeffery had decided not to work as a TA during the summer session. Otherwise he might have been stuck working with the duplicitous prick a few months longer.

"Why would you do this? You had third pick and we clicked, dammit."

Ty swallowed back the retort that wanted to spring from his lips, because Jeffery had clicked much better with Preston. "You know I can't confirm or deny what order we picked teaching assistants."

Dr. Carscadden had very particular ideas about how to run his department, and one of the most hated policies was the TA lottery. In random order, professors submitted their top three picks for TAs from the available pool of eligible grad students who applied each session. Professors with seniority despised it, and mocked the department head's reasons of preventing complacency and giving more students opportunities. Ty had never minded it—even though he was the newest professor in the department, he'd never ended up picking last, which meant he benefited by the lottery, now more than ever. The lottery order, though, was probably the worst kept secret in the department.

"There's no reason I should have gotten stuck with cranky Carscadden. He was almost last!" Jeffery pounded his fist on the desk and if he weren't so irate, Ty might have grinned. As the head of the department and the professor with the most seniority, Dr. Carscadden taught the fewest classes—his hatred of teaching first year classes another poorly kept secret—but somehow his TAs ended up being the most overworked and subject to the most intense performance reviews.

"Ty. You have to fix this." Jeffery pounded both hands on his desk this time, looking a little wild around the eyes.

"Jeffery, I don't know why you're so upset. I thought you wanted to work with Dr. Carscadden."

Ironically, when Ty had first chosen Jeffery, Jeffrey had been upset, wanting to work with Dr. Carscadden instead of the lowly Dr. Williams, but Dr. Carscadden never broke in an inexperienced TA if he could avoid it. Ty knew Jeffery hadn't been on Wendy's list of options, but he wasn't surprised Dr. Carscadden chose Jeffery. After all, Ty had been very careful not to talk about the incident at the Christmas party, after swearing Wendy to secrecy. He had no wish to be the subject of pitying speculation, nor did he think besmirching Jeffery's professional career an appropriate punishment. Spending the school year at Dr. Carscadden's beck and call? That was punishment fitting the crime.

Nevertheless, Jeffery's demands were as annoying as they were unnerving.

"Working for cranky Carscadden means I'll never have a free minute to..." Jeffery broke off, as though searching for the right words.

Fuck this. Ty filled in the blanks. "You'll never have what? Enough free time to cater to Preston's demands?"

Jeffery's mouth fell open as a flush rose up his throat and into his cheeks. "I was going to tell you. I mean, you guys broke up."

Ty snorted. "Yes. We broke up. Because I saw him fucking you at the faculty Christmas party. In the coat check. Rather tasteless, don't you think?"

Jeffery sputtered, "But you never said anything!"

"Of course I didn't say anything, you idiot. I was stuck working with you for the entire spring term. But the fates must have known what was in store, because you already knew you weren't going to work the summer session, so I was free to choose another TA. And she's done such a great job, I didn't see any reason not to choose her again. And at least Dr. Carscadden doesn't have to worry about you fucking his wife."

Jeffery gasped and his hands clenched into fists. This time there was no fear. He wasn't about to start a brawl in the middle of the university, but he was done sucking it up. He'd had to swallow his pride and anger for far too long, and the dam was broken.

"So, Jeffery, I think it's time for you to leave."

Jeffery took a step back, as he appeared to be completely unprepared to take responsibility for his actions.

"Oh, and Jeffery? Be prepared to work your ass off for Dr. Carscadden. Because if he finds your work unsatisfactory and asks why I didn't have you on my list for the lottery? I'll tell him the truth."

This time, Jeffery's face went paper white before he whirled and ran out of the office. Ty took a couple of deep breaths, fingers trembling from the stress.

"Um, Dr. Williams?"

Ty jumped at the unexpected voice. "Oh. Allison. I thought you'd left." He sank back down into his desk chair, legs just a bit too rubbery to remain standing.

"I... well, I got the call from Human Resources just before I got on the bus that I'd be working for you again and I wanted to come back and thank you. Did Jeffery really do that?"

God. He should have shut the door before having that confrontation with Jeffery. "Yes, I'm afraid so. But please keep it quiet. I don't want everyone talking about it."

Allison tsked. "Of course. But that's just terrible. I can't believe all spring you acted like nothing was wrong. I mean, aside from having broken up with your boyfriend."

Award winning acting, no doubt about it. "It was for the best. Truly." It had been a shocking betrayal, from both of them, but he'd never loved either of them, and even if the only man he was interested in sleeping with right now was a two-dimensional painted figure, it was still better than sleeping with that louse, Preston.

"Okay, well, I'll see you tomorrow?"

"Why wouldn't you?"

Allison winked at him. "Dunno. Sounded today like your throat was a little scratchy in that last lecture. If you maybe weren't feeling well tomorrow, I could cover your classes."

Ty smiled, although it was half-hearted at best. "Thank you, but I think I'll be fine." This was the sort of loyalty he could get behind.

"Good night." Allison left, her footsteps fading away.

Unfortunately, Ty couldn't shake his unease. Most likely he was simply reacting to enduring an unpleasant confrontation without adequate preparation. But, he hadn't actually expected Jeffery to be so angry, especially since it wasn't like Ty had prevented him from getting a TA position.

The trembling had ceased, but he still pulled out his phone. Craig would know if he was overreacting.

Ten minutes later, after most of his time was spent trying to convince Craig there wasn't anything to worry about, Ty heard the distinctive clack of high heeled shoes heading toward his office. Not everyone wore sensible footwear on campus, but he rather suspected he knew who owned those shoes. And she was the perfect excuse.

"Look, Craig, I gotta go. Work calls. But I promise I'll keep an eye out and call you if anything seems off."

Craig merely grunted in his ear, but it was probably as close as he'd get to assent. He disconnected and dropped the phone in his messenger bag.

Wendy burst into his office. "Oh, good, you're still here. They're making the calls to the TAs today. Just wanted to warn you."

Ty scrubbed his face with his hands. "Uh, yeah. Managed to figure that out."

"You did? Well, what about..." Wendy didn't bother finishing her sentence, but pursed her cotton candy pink lips and peered at Ty. "By all the saints, you've already heard from that little worm, haven't you?"

"Worse. He already showed up."

"He showed up here? I must have just missed him. What did he say?"

"I'm surprised you didn't hear the yelling." Wendy's office wasn't all that far from Ty's. "He wanted to know why I hadn't picked him. So I told him the truth."

"Shut the fuck up!" Wendy slapped the desk and collapsed into one of the chairs reserved for guests in his office. "And then what?"

Ty shrugged. "Nothing really. I mean, what could he say? Although I gathered that he and Preston are an item now."

"They deserve each other."

Which reminded him. "Carscadden hired him."

There was silence for a few seconds before Wendy started laughing. "Oh my God. If that isn't immediate karmic retribution, I don't know what is. It couldn't happen to a nicer fellow."

Although he laughed along with her, he wished Preston might get his own comeuppance. The universe didn't keep score, though, so Preston was likely going to continue on as he had. Someone once said the best revenge was living well, and Ty was working on that part. That was all Ty could control.

Wendy sucked in a deep breath and wiped at her eyes. "You have to let me take you out for a drink to celebrate."

"I don't know." He was glad the confrontation was over, but he wasn't sure he was at the point of jubilation. Yet.

"I insist. It's been too long since we've gone out and if you're not careful you're going to turn into a tweed-jacketed stick in the mud. Fortunately, you have me to keep you young, at least until you find yourself a boy toy."

Ty's cheeks heated. Even at forty-five Wendy was quite a bit more youthful than Ty, especially lately, but at least he didn't have to worry about Wendy setting him up with a dud. If nothing else, she had better taste in gay men than Ty's sister, but she also wasn't in a hurry to get him a boyfriend either, boy-toy comment notwithstanding. Of the two of them, Wendy was the most likely to end up with a boy toy.

"C'mon. Happy hour at the Rebel House."

"The Rebel House? Isn't that kind of far?" He certainly couldn't tell Wendy he wanted to go home and tell Max about this new development. That would just make Wendy redouble her efforts to make sure he wasn't lonely.

"Oh my God, princess, no. It's just a couple of subway stops. Unless you've scoped out a better spot near your new place. Which I haven't seen yet. Or did you want to head into boystown?"

"No gay bars. I don't need your help to get laid." Maybe she was worse than Mandy. There was a little pub not far from his place that he'd been meaning to check out, but taking Wendy back to his new apartment? No way was he ready for that. He didn't even want to know what Wendy would say about Max. "Uh, I haven't finished unpacking or anything. Rebel House is fine."

"Awesome. Let me grab my purse, and we can head out. We can discuss the date of your housewarming party."

Somehow he didn't think he was going to get out of the housewarming party, but he could delay it for a long while. He hoped. He'd already shared Max with more people than he really wanted to.

CHAPTER FOUR

"Allison kindly suggested I might want to call in sick today. But I only had the one lecture so I decided to go in just for that and take an early Friday." Ty looked directly at him, yet another thing he appreciated about Ty. This was more than Ty just talking to himself. "I'm already behind, so what's another half day? Besides, I'm dying to get into these newspaper articles, and I never thought I'd hear myself say that."

Max was content just to watch and listen. Ty had gotten in late enough last night that he'd merely tumbled into bed and fell asleep. But he'd explained what had happened at the university the previous day, which was yet another thing Max appreciated, even Ty had no idea Max was able to understand and sympathize with everything he'd said. The whole situation was not anything Max had direct experience with, but it certainly confirmed that these were very different times from those he'd lived in. He also didn't care how attractive this Jeffery person was, Preston had to have been an idiot to lose Ty over foolish behavior.

Silence fell over the room as Ty clicked keys on his laptop, pausing only occasionally to sip at a dark carbonated beverage. He wasn't sure if it was cola or root beer, but it brought back some happy memories of his years at the university whenever he could spare a few coins. He did prefer a root beer float, although that was an extravagance he'd only indulged in a few times. The ability to buy simple luxuries had been the first to go once the depression took hold, and Victor's sponsorship had never led to wealth. At least not for him.

After a couple of hours, Ty leaned back in his chair.

"These articles are pretty sensationalistic. Your name only appears once, that I can find, but you're described fairly often. They're sure quick to revile Victor, though."

Max knew that. Many people had hated Victor simply for how rich he was. The stock market crash had barely touched him. And since he was what many considered an abomination, very few found him worthy of admiration. Ty peered back at the computer screen and snorted.

"The occult? No way! *This* article speculates you were a sacrifice in a pagan ceremony. Where did they get this stuff? No one seriously believed that, did they?"

They did. Victor had three obsessions: fucking men on his own terms, getting into the elite art circle, and a fascination with the supernatural. Some called him the devil's spawn. Max didn't know if Victor had believed the supernatural would assist him in getting what he wanted or if it was an unconnected obsession.

"Huh." Tyler stretched out his fingers for a few moments. "These journalists were willing to crucify Victor for just about anything, rather than trying to seek justice for you, Max. I'm half expecting to see a claim he caused crops to wither or livestock to die, like the Salem witch trials.

"It seems strange to me that your whereabouts isn't one of those great mysteries, like the Bermuda Triangle or El Dorado's missing treasure, but then, I guess a lot of people slipped through the cracks during that time. Those with no family, anyway. I'm sorry that had to happen to you."

Tyler turned around in his chair to look Max in the eye. His sincerity humbled Max.

A horrific buzz made Ty jump and look around guiltily, even though Ty knew no one was around to see his little monologue to Max.

"That's awful, isn't it?" It was the first time he'd experienced the older style manual buzzer for guests. His previous apartment had a system that hooked up to his phone number, whether it be landline or mobile, but the older building had an archaic system that might be older than Ty himself. He tilted his head. Maybe this very building had been around in Max's day. He'd have to add that to his many avenues of exploration into a far more modern history than he was accustomed to researching.

"But since I'm not even supposed to be home from work, and I'm not expecting anyone, I think I'll just ignore that. I wouldn't put it past Jeffery to have looked up my home address and come back to argue his case again." Ty shivered just a bit. He didn't really think Jeffery was that tenacious, but neither had he expected the anger Jeffery had displayed in his office yesterday. That's what came of seeking comfort from Craig. As a cop, he saw the worst outcomes of altercations gone too far all the time, but he'd only succeeding in freaking Ty out, even as he'd managed to convince himself—mostly—that Jeffery wasn't a raving lunatic.

He'd just flipped to another newspaper—the search algorithms weren't nearly as useful as he'd expected, which may or may not be user error, when a sharp knock came at his door.

God. Had someone else in the building let the visitor in? They must have. Couldn't be his sister. Even her ham-handed attempts to set him up weren't pressing enough for her to interrupt her workday.

Unease fluttered in his belly. Surely it couldn't be Jeffery. Ty pushed back from his chair and padded out to the front door, trying to be as silent as possible. He wanted to maintain the illusion he wasn't at home, if possible. Peering through the peephole revealed no one. But this nervousness wasn't really like him. He flung open the door. No one stood outside, and Ty exhaled noisily. He was just about to shut the door again when he noticed the slim cardboard package on the ground, nestled up against the doorframe.

"Hey, Max! Look what came today." Ty waggled the package. "Antoine's memoirs. They'd given such a wide range for the estimated ship date, I assumed it would show up nearer the end of the range rather than the beginning." Going through Antoine's memoirs meant he could ditch the tedious newspaper research for a bit. Every piece of new information was a treat, but he despised research that involved newspapers.

He curled up into his oversized chair, opened the box, and pulled out the brightly colored book.

Flipping quickly through the book, he paused at the attractive, glossy photos. There were a lot more photos than text—not unexpected from a memoir of someone whose life focused more on the visual than anything else. Antoine LaRose was someone Ty had heard of, usually in the tabloids. Was it a coincidence this book hadn't been published until after Victor Cranston's death? Maybe, maybe not.

"He's good. Apparently Antoine did a lot of tattoo art in addition to his painting. Some of these are pretty cool." Ty turned another page.

"And some are graphic. More graphic than you, even." A few of the images were far closer to porn than Max's beautiful portrait. The next page, though, had Ty crossing his legs in a protective gesture.

"Holy shit, Max. Check it out!" Ty flipped the picture toward Max, resolutely ignoring the fact that Max wasn't real. "A tattooed dick. That had to have hurt." It was well done, but the pain couldn't be worth it. Not on his dick. He could manage a tattoo somewhere else, but he wasn't too creative and didn't want the same old hackneyed images everyone else had.

He didn't find any photos of Max, but it made sense in a way. If the painting was a killer's sick trophy, as Craig suspected, Victor wouldn't want it photographed.

Time to get down to work. Ty checked the table of contents. No reference to Victor or Max. He flipped to the back. No index. Damn.

Back at the table of contents, Ty found the page for Antoine's exploits in the eighties and began to read. After several minutes, he found what he was looking for.

"Here it is. Oh. It's short." Ty shouldn't be disappointed, but he was. He didn't even know what he expected to get out of the book, since the bits he'd read so far made Antoine seem like a shallow, oversexed guy far more interested in money than love. To be fair, Ty had met his fair share of single gay guys who had similar outlooks. Maybe that was why he'd been too quick to believe in his relationship, blind to the infidelity—because he'd wanted to believe Preston was different.

Ty opened his mouth. Closed it. God. He really was crazy, but he started to read aloud anyway.

1981

Victor Cranston was my first sponsor. He wasn't respected in art circles, but he was wealthy, he knew wealthy art buyers, he wanted to fuck me, and he didn't care that I had a criminal record. How could he? The man was nuts. He was obsessed by the occult and kept threatening to put curses on anyone who betrayed him. I needed his connections, and he needed the tight ass I waggled at him. He was mostly harmless, though, and he had an extensive art collection. His erratic and self-indulgent behavior meant he only ever hovered on the fringes, never truly welcome, and even a good eye for quality couldn't overcome that.

He owned this enormous painting of the lover he supposedly murdered, like, fifty years before. A guy named Maxwell Friedland, another painter he'd sponsored. The painting was fabulous. As was Maxwell. Nude, trim, and hung like a horse. I don't know what Victor was thinking; I sure wouldn't have killed anyone with a dick like that. In fact, I thanked all the saints looking after starving artists that Victor kept the painting in the bedroom. It was the only way I could pretend to enjoy Victor's swift and selfish fucking.

Ty lifted his head from the book to speak to Max. "Doesn't sound like Victor was the only selfish one in that bed. I wasn't expecting him to be so graphic about it. I hope..." Ty sure as hell didn't want to say it aloud. Was there a difference between Ty letting Max fuel his masturbatory fantasies and a guy who used Max to fool someone else? He hoped so. He didn't want anyone, Max included, to think he considered Max the piece of meat Antoine described in his memoir. The way Antoine wrote about Max made him very uncomfortable; he wasn't like Antoine, was he? He shook his head and went back to the memoir.

I asked Victor several times during our two years together if he'd killed Maxwell. How cool would it be to get that confirmed? By the end, I was more interested in knowing the truth about the murder than anything else Victor could give me.

Ty snickered. Yeah, right. It was obvious Antoine had only been interested in one thing Victor gave him: money.

"What do you think, Max? Were you really the reason Antoine stayed so long? Somehow I don't think so." Did Preston believe money would keep men in his bed? He'd certainly never offered any to Ty, and if he had, their relationship would have been over all the sooner. A relieved laugh escaped. Ty was nothing like Antoine, but he could see a lot of similarities between Victor and Preston. Antoine's phrase "selfish fucking" resonated—an apt description for someone who couldn't even keep it in his pants while at his boyfriend's faculty Christmas party.

"There's just a bit more."

> *Victor often said the painting was the greatest trompe l'oeil the world had ever known. Then he'd laugh. I never saw the trick—I have no idea what Victor meant. He also claimed to have painted it, but the quality was too good. Someone with that kind of talent wouldn't stop at one kinky painting of a dead lover. Sometimes, though, I'd catch him talking to it, like it was a person. Victor was quite mad. Dumping him for Anwar was the best thing I ever did.*

"Well, Max, if there was any evidence Antoine was a gold-digger, that was it. You wouldn't know, but Anwar Saffic's net worth was probably triple Victor's."

Everyone who was alive in the eighties and nineties was aware of Antoine's tempestuous relationship with the playboy billionaire. The affair launched Antoine's art career into superstar status, and the resulting twenty-year affair played out for the public in the tabloids.

But *trompe l'oeil*? It was an art term, meant "optical illusion" or, more literally, "trick the eye." Ty had seen it employed in historic European churches to create the illusion of domes and height on the ceilings. It became common in the Renaissance and Baroque periods, but even those eras were a little late for him.

"I don't see it either. What did Victor mean?" No trick of perception leaped out. "I guess I shouldn't feel too bad since Antoine was an artist and he couldn't see the illusion either."

Ty set the book aside and walked over to Max. Being close made him wish Max's beautiful face and body were real and here and his. He shoved the quiver of lust away in favor of inspecting Max's painting.

"Was it the fact you seem to reflect my mood? Did that happen with Victor?" He couldn't shake the notion but recognized its idiocy. Like the way people thought the eyes of a painting followed them around the room.

Trying to assess the painting dispassionately, he cleared his mind and started at the top, working his way down. Around Max's neck was a short necklace, choker-style, with a polished, carved stone pendant. It looked antique, maybe ancient, and reminded Ty of something he'd seen before. He grabbed his phone and snagged a close-up photo of it to study later. Besides being a point of interest, the necklace didn't qualify as a *trompe l'oeil*, so Ty continued his perusal, dropping to his knees to avoid straining his back.

Other than a stunning attention to detail, Ty didn't see anything unusual until he got to Max's groin...er, wrists. The more he looked at Max's fucking gorgeous erect cock, the more distracting it became. He yearned to know the heft of it in his hand, the taste of it on his tongue, how well it would fill him up, in either mouth or ass, the sensation of it thrusting home in his body. Ty's cock filled with blood while his ass clenched in futile sympathy.

Tempting as it was to take out his dick and start stroking, that's not what he was there to do. Once he took his focus off Max's incredible dick—and he barely kept himself from touching it—he noticed a subtle difference in the bed sheets Max was sprawled in. Ty reached out a fingertip and stroked the anomaly. Brushing his fingers over the paint didn't help him see better, but he couldn't stop.

"Are those shackles? Restraints of some kind?"

Ty stared up into Max's face, wished he had the answers, tried to avoid imagining kneeling like this in front of a naked Max in the flesh. Was this evidence of some kink of Max's? Had Max not wanted to pose? Or was it merely some fantasy of Victor's incorporated into the painting? Perhaps it was a subtle reference to the subservience a man like Max would have been expected to show someone like Victor.

Ty rocked back on his heels. "Whether you liked to be tied up or not—and I have to say, under the right circumstances, it could be fun..." Ty didn't bother saying he'd enjoy it if Max were to tie him up and make him plead for Max's fat prick. The sudden influx of blood to his cock seconded the notion.

"But I don't believe—whatever happened—you were happy with Victor. I can't believe it." Not that he had any basis for that belief, aside from the sadness in Max's expression. "Victor seems a lot like Preston: entitled, wealthy, and a complete shit. Except for Antoine, I can't imagine any artist hoping for a sponsor would be interested in a man like that."

A repeat of the harsh buzz made Tyler flinch, drawing his attention away from Max's groin. *Neiiiin.* Tyler had been going to touch his erection; he was sure of it. Max swore Tyler's fingertips touched his wrists. Under Tyler's intense perusal, the prison wall grew tacky where Max had pressed up against it. Having Tyler poised on the floor, as though ready to take Max's cock into his mouth, was indescribable.

"Shit. Who could that be?" Tyler stood with a grunt and left the bedroom.

The murmur of a woman's voice joined Tyler's. Max tried to squelch his jealousy. It was a useless, futile emotion, one he had no right to feel. Besides his growing affection and desire for Tyler, he wanted to be able to talk to him. His inability to respond to Tyler spiked his temper like little else in recent memory.

"Mandy, I'm fine." Tyler led the way back into the bedroom.

Max relaxed. Staying in the bedroom meant he'd still hear and see Tyler.

"And even if I wasn't, I'm too old to have my best friend tattling to my big sister. Jeffery's harmless."

Max agreed. Considering the stories Tyler had told him, his upset was justified. Unfortunate but justified. Every word Tyler spoke encouraged Max's growing belief that parts of society accepted gay men and gay relationships and gay breakups. The heartache might be worth experiencing that freedom.

Mandy burst into the room behind Tyler, carrying a box that had seen better days. It looked nothing like the almost pristine cardboard boxes Tyler was unpacking. In fact, the box looked like it had been moldering, forgotten, in an attic for several years. Possibly longer than Tyler had been alive.

"Well, Craig was worried about you. And he squealed to Jake, who tattled to me. Get it right. Oh, hello..." Mandy directed her last words at Max. An all too common reaction to him—when they didn't gasp and make the sign of the cross, anyway.

"I outdid myself with that one." Mandy looked him up and down before placing the mangy box on the desk.

"For God's sake, quit drooling over my painting. If that's all you came here for, you can leave. As you can see, I've still got a lot of unpacking to do."

"Ungrateful brat." The smile softened her words, and the tone couldn't be mistaken for anything but caring. Mandy grabbed Tyler's chin and peered into his eyes. "Did you go out last night?"

"No. Why?"

"Were you drinking last night? Alone?"

"I went to the Rebel House with Wendy." Given Ty's almost defiant tone, the name of the pub was appropriate.

Mandy sniffed. "A straight bar with a woman. That's not going to get you laid. Or back on the horse." She winked. "Or both?"

Ty's sharp cheekbones developed a faint wash of pink. Obviously, Tyler wasn't going to tell his sister everything. Max knew his own sisters would have been worried about him in the same situation, but sometimes the occasion just called for getting drunk. Tyler deserved that release every now and then, although when he'd returned the previous night he'd merely been tipsy.

"Oh, Tyler." Mandy pulled her brother into a hug, which he returned, but he rolled his eyes. "You know I just want you to be happy. But you do realize that just having a sex cave isn't good enough. You need to actually let other sexy studs know about it."

Sex cave?

Tyler's cheeks pinkened further as he pulled out of her arms. "Shut up."

"Why? No one's around to hear about your wild sex parties."

Sex parties? Max's stomach plummeted to the vicinity of his lower frame. Tyler's compassion for Max set him miles apart from Victor. Was Max wrong about Tyler's true nature?

"Mandy!" Max was familiar with that tone—he'd used it more than once when his sisters had teased him. Relief swelled; he hadn't been wrong about Tyler.

"Oh, hush. If only you were that exciting. I know your first instinct is to hide like a recluse. But you need to get out, meet people. Meet a man who's not a rat like Preston."

"Can we not talk about this? I was an idiot. I get it. But you could have called to tell me that."

"Oh, right. Well, I can't believe I found this so quick. Fate or something, considering how much crap Victor Cranston had in his house. I swear, that man's basement was a hoarder's wet dream. But like the penis painting, Cranston's heirs wanted nothing to do with this." Mandy thrust the box at Tyler. Max wished desperately he could rip open the box. He wanted to know what was inside.

Tyler moved his laptop aside and took the box from Mandy to place it on the desk. He wiped away some of the grime on top and scrubbed his fingers clean on his jogging pants. "It says *Maxwell.*"

Maxwell? As in, well, him? *Tyler, open the damned box.* Max tried yelling again, but it didn't work.

"I know what it says. That's why I brought it over. Thought you'd be interested."

Tyler stared at the box, making no move to open it.

Mandy threw up her hands. "God, you're annoying. Even as a kid, you'd never rip the paper off your gifts. You had to examine them, open them as though there were bombs inside. Sometimes I can't believe you're my brother. Forget it. I can't hang around here all night. Jake and I are going out for dinner. Date night!" Mandy sang the last two words with a leer.

"Okay, well, bye." The box totally absorbed Tyler's attention; he didn't even look at Mandy while she spoke. Max understood her exasperation. He wanted Tyler to rip open the box too. But despite her words, Mandy didn't appear to be in any hurry to leave.

"You know, Ty, there's a guy who started working at the spa across the street --"

"No."

"Why? What's wrong with going out on a date?"

Date? Out in public? With another man? Max still found it incredible that gay men truly did that in this day and age. Much less with the encouragement of—some—family and friends. Max hadn't believed Victor when he'd mentioned as much, but then, Max wouldn't let Victor convince him water was wet. Not after decades of imprisonment.

"Hey, look at me." Mandy pulled her brother away from his intense inspection of the carton, which was, amazingly, still unopened.

"I don't want to go on some blind date. You have terrible taste in gay men."

Good. Max didn't want Tyler to go out on a blind date either.

"He's cute. Nice butt. You don't have to marry the guy, but you need to get laid."

Tyler flicked a glance over at him, and the slight flush intensified. Max's laugh echoed through his head; Tyler was thinking about jerking off to Max.

Wait, had Mandy said *married*? She must have been exaggerating. Dating publicly, maybe. Marriage? Impossible. Society couldn't have changed *that* much.

"Whacking off to Mr. Hung over there doesn't count as getting laid."

Maybe not, but it was as close to getting laid—a term Max had picked up since being in the painting—as Max had been in decades.

"I don't want to talk about this with my sister! Most people don't want to know about their siblings' sex lives. I don't." Tyler raked fingers through his hair, but he continued to flick glances at Max. Max wasn't great at flirting, but he had a come-hither look he'd like to give Tyler. One Tyler wouldn't be able to mistake for anything other than desire. Max wished they'd stop talking about Tyler getting laid. He was more than content for Tyler to stroke off with Max as inspiration. He couldn't remember sex ever giving him as much joy as watching Tyler in his solitary enjoyment did.

"Fine. Don't go out with him. But go out. Try. Preston isn't worth this kind of angst. He wasn't worth six days of it, never mind six months. Your birthday is coming up and you want to celebrate with a bang, right?"

Preston. Max wanted to hug Tyler, comfort him for the hurt Preston had caused. Max scratched at the confines of his prison. Instead of the usual lack of feeling, the canvas clung to his fingers like linseed oil, but he didn't know what that meant.

Ty groaned. "I'm having dinner at your place with you, Jake, and Craig. I'm not sure Craig would be up for being the party favor."

Mandy laughed.

"Seriously, sis. I'm not still hung up on Pres. How many times do I have to tell people that?"

"Words don't mean much—actions are what count. And right now, you're acting like you're still heartbroken."

Tyler ground his teeth together. Max wondered why no one took Tyler at his word. "I never loved Preston."

Mandy crossed her arms and tapped a foot. "Okay, then. Prove it. This city has such a large gay population, you ought to take advantage of it." She made a shooing motion.

"What? I'm supposed to leave right now? Offer to suck the first cock I come across?"

The siblings stood in front of each other, poses reflecting their irritation. It was amusing, as much as Max wanted to step between them and break it up.

"No. But soon. Tonight? This weekend? Next? If you don't do something, I'll be forced to. But make sure you shower first because you reek." Mandy pinched her nose and twisted her lips into an exaggerated grimace.

With the threat and insult hanging in the air, Mandy flounced out of the room. Tyler called after her, "Thanks for the box."

Polite words, but the tone was angry. Mandy couldn't have missed it.

"You're welcome, shithead," floated back to the bedroom.

Tyler sniffed, and as soon as the door slammed shut, he pivoted toward Max. "Well, now you've seen how childish I am."

No, not childish. All man. With a sister. Max understood.

"She wasn't kidding about drastic measures, though. When she gave you to me, I was seriously afraid she'd gotten me a prostitute."

Tyler didn't—shouldn't—have to pay for it. Not with his looks.

"And if I don't at least look like I'm trying, that's probably what she'll do." Tyler shuddered a little. Max agreed. There was something a bit unsavory about paying for sex, especially since he'd witnessed Victor doing so much of it. Even when Victor was young and good-looking, he'd used his wealth to attract those who'd fuck him for a small slice of it. Max was the only one who couldn't be bought—and he was also the only one trapped in a damned painting.

"At the very least, she'll give spa guy my address and phone number." Tyler ran his fingers lightly over the grubby box before he sighed and rummaged through the clothes he'd left on the floor last night. He pulled out the smooth, flat camera he'd used to take a picture of the necklace around Max's neck and swiped a finger along the slick surface.

"Darren, hi, it's Ty."

It was a telephone too. If Max had breath, he might have gasped. The technology of Tyler's world was incredible. Victor's phones had gotten bigger and bigger, but his eyesight began failing as he got older. Max had seen mobile phones in some of the sitcoms Victor had been addicted to in his later years and they'd been remarkable enough, but there had clearly been huge strides in the technology since Victor's death. Even before, there was much Victor hadn't shown him. But then, it wasn't like Victor was his tour guide to the twenty-first century. He'd been a vicious beast more concerned with taunting Max whenever he could. At least until the end, when he'd become lonely enough not to try and piss Max off. Between labored breaths and extended naps, he'd talked almost constantly to Max.

"Yeah, well, I'm not unpacked yet, but I could use a break. You going anywhere fun tonight?"

Tyler paused for a moment. Max watched him stride to his closet and flip one-handed through the shirts hanging there.

"Right. Ten. Perfect. See you then."

Tyler tapped the phone and slid it back on his desk before turning back to Max. "Hopefully that will be enough to satisfy her." His nose twitched. "I guess I do need a shower."

Who was this Darren fellow? Was Tyler going on a date with him? Jealousy gnawed at Max again, completely unlike the sickening feeling he'd gotten watching Victor with his many conquests; this was something else. No matter how foolish it was, he feared he was destined to endure this every time Tyler went out.

"It's been a long time since I've gone dancing. Maybe it will be fun." Tyler didn't look or sound convinced. He glanced at his watch and grimaced, then looked at Max again. "But this means I won't have time to open the box. What have you got hidden in there, I wonder?"

Ja, Max wondered that too. He was amazed Victor had kept anything of his—Max's belongings would have been worth less than nothing to the incredibly rich Victor Cranston.

Shoulders slumped, Tyler searched through suitcases, presumably looking for something to wear. What did men in this day and age wear dancing? Was he going to dance with men or women?

After another meal of leftover pizza—Craig would kill him if he knew—Tyler couldn't stop speculating about what was in the tempting, enticing *Maxwell* box. He sighed, so close to bailing on his plans with Darren and the other guys. That was the problem with making plans for ten at night. Gave him far too long to waffle about his decision, and wonder if he was getting just too old for this nonsense. But if he wanted Mandy and Craig off his back, and to get a start on his new, single, sex-filled lifestyle, he needed to get out of his damn apartment. Sex without strings was a good idea, wasn't it? If only he didn't feel so comfortable at home with Max.

He tossed a shirt and pair of pants on the bed. They were clean, mostly club-worthy, and he wouldn't even have to locate his iron. The club they were going to wasn't super fancy, nor was it a full on meat market, but more like a bar with decent music and a dance floor. He wouldn't need his best club wear, but Darren would taunt him endlessly and forever if he showed up dressed like he was going to work or something. Darren would trot out some teasing tirade about living up to his reputation as a gay man, how Ty was adversely affecting Darren's chances to find a decent piece of tail... Darren was the most aggressively single person Ty knew, and a good friend.

"Okay, Max, got to get myself in the mood. At least it's a club I'm familiar with. Much better for getting my feet wet."

Tyler puttered around, trying to find a few things from specific boxes. Maybe Mandy was right. If he'd been himself, his apartment would be completely unpacked by now, and he wouldn't be searching for the portable speaker dock for his phone. At least he hadn't opened Max's box. If he had, he'd never be ready in time to meet Darren.

"Here it is." Tyler tore into the box he was looking for. No matter what Mandy thought, he wasn't meticulous with everything, just those things that mattered to him.

"Max, you're going to get an education in modern music." Tyler hefted the phone in his hand. "Well, maybe not totally modern. But it's stuff I like, and it's way more modern than the last time you went dancing. Ought to help me get ready for tonight." Ty gave his hips an experimental shimmy. "Haven't been dancing since I started dating Preston. He said he didn't like it, but now I wonder if he lied about that too. Maybe he went dancing with one of his boys on the side when I thought he was out working."

That alone was enough to convince Ty to go out. Damn Preston, taking away something Ty liked.

"Maybe tonight I can find a guy live and in person, and not using an app." Ty frowned at Max. So much in the world had changed since Max had lived.

"I wonder what you'd even think about that. I mean, you've got that gorgeous dick on display, so I don't think you could have been prudish. Or maybe this is merely someone's fantasy. But these days, we've got things called apps. It helps us find people near us interested in the same things. Mostly though, it's used to find hookups—no strings sex—which means it's flooded with dick pics. I'm not a huge fan, although I do love your picture." Ty waggled his phone and slid it onto his desk beside the speaker dock, not even tempted to open the app. He'd used it on occasion, sure, but he didn't get the appeal. Probably a side effect of spending so much time lost in the past.

He grabbed a towel and marched into the shower. Been a while since he prepared for a possible lover. He wasn't craving sex, but it would be nice if he had the option. He still looked good, but he was getting older and needed to put his best foot forward to have a fighting chance.

Max waited breathlessly for Ty to return, the concept of an Internet-thing flooded with images of dicks not fazing him at all. Since it was virtually the only thing Victor had ever used it for, Max wasn't surprised other people did as well. He just appreciated that Ty's interest in such a fascinating information source wasn't purely sexual. Max would love to get a chance to see how it all worked, after seeing the things Ty had been able to do with it.

Ty seemed to take a rather long time, but his patience was rewarded when Ty emerged from the bathroom in a cloud of steam, naked except for the towel around his waist.

Max had a sudden flash of memory. When he was in university, he'd debated visiting a bathhouse he'd heard about. He'd walked past the nondescript doorway several times, imagining it to be full of attractive men dressed as Tyler was now. But he'd never quite had the courage to go in—the element of secretiveness and potential tawdriness made him nervous. Shortly afterward, he'd been recalled home, and there was never money again for such frivolousness. Nothing in his imagination had anything on the water-slicked beauty standing before him. It wasn't the first time he'd seen Tyler in a similar state of undress, but it was a sight that never got old.

With the lithe grace of a dancer, Tyler moved across the room to the "speaker dock" device, plugged it into the wall, and inserted the flat phone into a slot.

Harsh rhythmic sounds swelled and filled the room. Max would have jumped had he been able, but from the look of almost bliss on Tyler's face, he enjoyed the strange cacophony. Max was only able to understand about one in ten words, but every move Tyler made followed the underlying bass rhythm. Tyler writhed sinuously to the tunes, stimulating an awareness of how dark and sensual the music was. Of course, Max approved of anything that made Tyler move like he was in orgasmic bliss—or about to get fucked.

Tyler pulled on some pants, much to Max's dismay. Until he saw how tight they were. Max swallowed. The pants drew the eye directly to Tyler's crotch. His lean, nude torso rose above the pants, and if Max could have begged him not to go out, he would have. With Tyler actively looking for a little action, he couldn't fail to find it. Without underwear, everything would be easy access.

Ty swayed in front of Max, giving him a show. "The pants still fit, don't they?"

Well, yes, if mouthwateringly indecent was the look he was going for.

Tyler took a break from taunting Max to look in his dresser mirror, which was propped up against the wall by the closet. As he watched himself, he tweaked his small nipples to hardness and moaned softly. Max wanted to do that for him.

Tyler wasn't going out shirtless, was he?

"Dunno, Max. You think I'm maybe too skinny? Looks okay when I'm dressed, but naked? Oh well. I'll worry about that when I've had a drink or two."

No. Not too skinny. Perfect.

Tyler swiped up the crimson shirt he'd laid out on the bed, pulled it on, and buttoned it. Max could have painted a shirt on Tyler that wouldn't be as tight. He was gorgeous, and no one with eyes would be able to resist him. Dammit.

Frowning into the mirror, Tyler tilted his head. "Eh, Max, maybe not too old yet."

Wasn't too old for Max. Tyler was prime.

He disappeared through the door, and Max heard more rummaging and muffled cursing over the music.

Tyler dashed back into the room, snatched his phone from the speakers and inexplicably managed to wedge it into a back pocket. "Shit, I'm gonna be late."

Looking at Max one final time, he smiled. All the air sucked right out of Max's prison. Thick black eyeliner outlined Tyler's eyes, making them look even more exotic and alluring than ever, bringing out the gold flecks in his polychromatic eyes. Max's reaction upon seeing Antoine with eyeliner was a muted echo to the throbbing want and need thrumming through Max, like the music Tyler had danced to moments earlier. The hypnotic music and Tyler's mesmerizing movements were out of the realm of the familiar, but he liked it all. He liked Tyler, more than he should, dammit.

Max flailed against the canvas, wanting to kiss Tyler's smile, slide his tongue over those full lips, touch those raven-ringed eyes. Again, the impenetrable wall flexed under his frenzy. Was it merely a reflection of his desperation to touch Tyler? Was it madness? Max didn't know, but he pounded at the canvas with both fists while it sagged like bread dough under his assault. When Tyler flung him one last smile and softly whispered, "Good night," the wall of his prison sprang back, shoving him away. Max ran his fingers over it again, but there was no more give, no sticky spots like there had been before. Its customary glasslike surface had returned.

Ty made his way to the second-floor patio bar. His friends usually staked out a table between the bar and the covered dance floor. The music was loud but good. Ty's hips swayed a bit as he waited in line for a drink. It had been a long time since he'd gone out like this. Preston hated his friends—that should have been his first clue his relationship was headed for disaster. Reclaiming a bit of fun was a great way to start off this new chapter in his life.

For a change, he'd be able to walk home afterward, instead of either staying sober and driving or taking a long subway ride followed by a longer bus ride.

Ty laughed. Moving to his new apartment had been a damn good idea, for a number of reasons.

The bartender cupped a hand behind his ear when Ty made it to the bar.

"Two Long Islands," Ty yelled to be heard over the thumping bass. Within minutes, he had both hands full of booze, and he turned to the patio.

"Tyler! Over here." Darren waved, and Ty headed over. He set his drinks down in front of the only empty seat. Darren sprang up to hug him, and he waved at Raj and Simon.

"Two-fisting tonight?" Darren raised an eyebrow at the two large drinks.

Ty ignored the question. Tonight he vowed not to wallow. Otherwise he'd be at home, hip-deep in ice cream.

"Good for you." Darren patted his hand. "It's been too long since the four of us have been out."

Simon raised his glass, and the four of them clinked. Darren had collected the three of them nine years ago at this very club. Ty hadn't been in the closet, not in the clubs, but he hadn't considered himself totally out of the closet until he'd told his parents.

"Why didn't you bring that big brute, Craig, with you?" Darren fluttered his eyelashes, making the other guys laugh.

"Dare, you're a sexy guy, but you're never going to convert Craig." Never stopped him from trying though, and Ty appreciated Craig's good-natured response to Darren's flirting.

Darren stroked down his sides and wiggled in the chair. "Yeah, well, I still say I just need the right combination of booze and perfect outfit, and I'm in! Or he is!" Darren winked. "Speaking of...you planning to take someone home tonight?"

"Maybe. Why?" Darren knew Ty was typically reluctant to engage in one-night stands, although he'd never quite understood. His friend was a true believer in "if it feels good, why not?"

"It's a good night for it." Darren surreptitiously pointed out a number of attractive men who didn't appear attached.

Ty took a large mouthful of his drink as his friends commented on the attributes of the various men flowing in and out of the overheated club. Simon and Raj had been a couple almost since the day they'd met, and Ty had never known them to play around, so the exercise was academic for them.

Lucky bastards. Why hadn't he seen how unfaithful Preston was? He swallowed more booze, hoping it would fill up the emptiness inside. Darren would suggest grabbing one of these guys for a blowjob in the bathroom as his cure-all, but none of them, even the ones checking him out, appealed. He wasn't even missing Preston—he just missed what Preston represented.

"Hey." Darren nudged him with an elbow. "Drink up. I think we should do something more momentous to celebrate your return to the living."

If only Ty was as happy as Darren thought he should be. He'd come out. He'd ditched a cheating boyfriend. He had a great new apartment with a sex cave. He'd officially ditched Jeffery as a TA and he'd soon be up for tenure. His sister got him a gorgeous painting with a compelling research side project. Resolving to cheer up, Ty finished both of his drinks in quick succession. The dance floor began to wobble as his friends' faces got hazy.

"What did you have in mind?" Ty didn't think he was slurring. Yet. The night was still young.

Darren tapped a finger to his lips. "Tattoos? Piercings? You could get a Prince Albert."

"Jeez, Darren. Think about my dick much?"

Darren laughed delightedly. It had been a long time since Ty had been able to banter with his friends, but he hoped Darren wasn't serious. No amount of alcohol could convince him to pierce his dick. Or tattoo it, like the one he'd seen in Antoine's memoir.

"That's the Tyler I know and love. But seriously, you should do something."

Did he want to do this? He was a little old for this type of rebellion, wasn't he? Ty rubbed at his chest as he considered it.

"Nipples. Perfect." Darren grabbed his arm and pulled him out of his chair. "I know just the place, and they're open late."

"Wait! I don't know --"

"Yes, you do. You guys coming?" Darren asked the other two men.

"Nah, you two go ahead. Come back later and show us, though," Simon said with an exaggerated leer.

Ty might regret this tomorrow for more than just the hangover, but between Darren's enthusiasm and the amount of alcohol already swimming in his system, he didn't have the energy to fight back.

Darren steered him into the bedroom, sucking at his neck and rubbing his erection along Ty's hardness.

"Oh, lovey, we should have done this long ago," Darren whispered before thrusting his tongue into Ty's ear. Ty squirmed and panted.

Darren moved one hand off Ty's ass and flicked at the new ring in his nipple through his shirt.

Ty hissed. "Stop. It's too soon." The booze muted the pain enough to let some of the pleasure through. If he'd been sober, he'd have decked Darren.

"Spoilsport." Darren licked along Tyler's jaw to capture his lips.

Lack of air eventually made him dizzy. Ty pulled out of the kiss as the room spun.

"Let's take a look at your new digs, sweet. You said something about a sex cave?" Darren was steadier on his feet, so Ty tottered over to the bed as Darren turned on the light. Thankfully Tyler had had the sense not to put bright lights in the bedroom, or he'd be squinting.

"Oh, Tyler. Where have you been hiding him?"

Who? Ty followed Darren's leering gaze to Max.

"Where did you get this pretty piece?" Darren opened his pants, letting his erection spring out, and began stroking it.

"Mandy gave him to me as a housewarming gift."

"Well, she's got excellent taste." Darren continued to jack himself while staring at Max.

"Cut it out."

"What's the matter, lovey? God, he's got a great dick."

Ty didn't know where the possessiveness came from, but he still felt the need to protect Max—a painting—from lecherous stares and curious touches. He wasn't jealous of Max and his package. Was it what he'd already learned about Max?

Darren was a safe one-night stand and a nonthreatening way to ease into the new sexual-smorgasbord life Ty had hoped to begin, but tonight only convinced him he wasn't cut out for this. And watching Darren stroke off while reaching out to touch Max made Ty even more uncomfortable.

Near-sobriety returned in a rush as Ty leaped off the bed and grabbed Darren's hand before he could reach the canvas. "Don't touch him."

"Him? Darling, you're seriously delusional. But you're right. I shouldn't ignore you for the porn in the room, no matter how compelling."

That wasn't what he'd meant.

"Strip, darling, and you can fuck me." Darren aimed his hard dick at Ty.

Right. He'd forgotten Darren didn't top. Ty liked both, but right now he wanted to be done to, not the one doing. It had been too long, and he wanted to be taken care of, like he hadn't been since the early days with Preston. With shock, Ty realized his cock had completely deflated.

"Dare, I'm sorry."

Darren's black brows lifted to his hairline. "No strings, you know. It's been a long time for you, lovey. Have you forgotten how much fun it is?"

Six months. More. But Darren knew that. It was dirty pool to remind him of his dry spell. Still, Ty shook his head.

"Oh, darling. I gave up that blond for you." Darren's voice was full of reproach, but they'd been friends long enough, Ty didn't worry about irreparable damage to their friendship.

"Which blond?" Ty hadn't noticed Darren scoping out anyone in particular before convincing him to leave the club to get his nipples pierced.

Darren smirked at him. "Oh, any of them." He checked his watch. "I can still catch last call, if you're sure we're not doing this."

"No. Sorry." Was it appropriate to kiss Darren good-bye? They'd never kissed before tonight.

"Your loss, lovey."

"I know." Ty couldn't keep the smile out of his voice. "Thanks for tonight."

Darren tucked himself away with difficulty and leaned over the bed to kiss Ty. That answered that question. "No problem. But next time, I'm bringing someone else along, just in case." Darren grinned and blew him a kiss as he strutted out of the bedroom.

Ty laughed, even though he knew deep down this would never happen again. Darren made a great friend, but Ty didn't have his casualness regarding sex. The lack of strings had turned out to be a bigger problem for him than he'd ever imagined. His newfound resolution to approach sex differently was a big failure. Not surprising—he found sex too intimate to grant to strangers, except in cases of extreme horniness.

He lay back on the bed and listened to his apartment door close. Relief, sweet and silent, swept through him. His apartment had become a haven in a very short time. His apartment and Max. Tyler glanced over, trying desperately not to look at the package Darren and Antoine had been vocal about admiring. Why did it strike him as wrong when they did it but not when he did it? Whatever the reason, he didn't want to think about it. Tonight he could blame the alcohol, because if he considered it while totally sober, he might have to start seeing a psychiatrist.

Loud, raucous male laughter filtered in from the direction of his front door, waking Ty from his doze. Shit. He hadn't locked his door after Darren left. Stupid, especially downtown. Not that he was in a bad area, but no point in taking a risk.

Adrenaline chased away his fatigue, and his buzz remained, but muted. When he came back into his dimly lit room—he hadn't even turned off the light when he'd fallen asleep—the first sight he saw was Max. Biting his lip, he walked back to the kitchen and got his toolbox, small and pathetic though it was. He wasn't incapable of home maintenance, as Craig had implied more than once, but he wasn't a fan of it either.

"Hey, Max. Hope you don't mind if I move you." Had to be a trick of the light. Max looked more melancholy than he had since the day Mandy unwrapped him. Holy crap. Had that only been a few weeks ago? Max felt as much a part of his life as Craig and Mandy did. He was fucked up. But it was a harmless sort of fucked up, so Ty was going with it. University professors were supposed to be eccentric, weren't they?

He hoisted Max off his moorings, losing his footing for a moment when he discovered the painting was far heavier than expected. After propping Max gently against the dresser, he inspected what Craig had done to keep the painting firmly on the wall.

Within a few minutes, he'd recreated it on the wall at the foot of his bed. Should he wait for Craig? Ty was taller than Craig by a couple inches, but his friend was a lot stronger.

No. Asking Craig to help would get him an interrogation worthy of the worst criminal Craig had ever arrested. Or Craig would assume his motive was to make it easier to beat off to the sight of the painting. Having Max in his line of vision wouldn't adversely affect him getting off, but he didn't want Craig to think he was that lonely and pathetic. Never mind Craig was going to assume the worst the next time he saw the redecoration in Ty's bedroom but there was no point in inviting pity before he needed to.

It wasn't as easy as he'd hoped, but Ty managed to get Max seated properly on the wall without a drunken tilt.

Ty stepped back and surveyed his work. "That's much better." And it was. It was like he'd fixed a minor flaw in the room's feng shui. Even Max looked happier.

From the comfort of his bed, Ty was able to view the entire length of Max without straining his neck. Be a better view from his desk, too.

"You're so beautiful, you know. Everyone seems obsessed by your dick. Don't get me wrong—it's awesome, especially if it's true to life. But the rest of you is spectacular." If Victor had gone to the trouble of keeping this painting, why had he hung it at the head of the bed? Aside from the fact that Ty's ceilings didn't reach the lofty heights of the über-rich, why wouldn't Victor want to view this masterpiece from his bed?

"Tomorrow I'm going to find out more about you in that box, I hope." Ty gave his dick a halfhearted rub, but he was in the realm of the exhausted and drifted off, a smile on his face.

This time, Max hadn't imagined it. The canvas trapping him had moved, sluggishly. Seeing Tyler kiss another man made Max's ears burn hot enough he thought he'd set the painting on fire—and that was a disaster he didn't want to contemplate. He wanted to rip the small man away from Tyler's long body, sock him in the mouth, and stake a claim. Utterly ridiculous, since none of that could happen, but the jealousy was molten and intense. Not even when Tyler described his breakup with that fool, Preston, had it been this overwhelming. Because who could be jealous of the idiot who let Tyler get away? Angry on his behalf, yes, because Max wanted Tyler to be happy all the time. But the raging, blinding possessiveness was new.

Desperate pounding on the wall of his prison garnered him exactly zero attention from the couple kissing sloppily on the bed, as did screaming his throat raw. He'd never had this reaction in all the years in Victor's ownership, but for the first time in decades, Max wanted someone, and horror of horrors, he was going to have to watch another man take what he wanted. When Tyler finally sent Darren on his way with nothing more than a few kisses, Max sagged back in relief. While Tyler dozed fully dressed, Max lifted a hand, wishing to touch him. The canvas was again glassy and cold, and Max pressed his forehead to it in frustration. Tyler woke suddenly a few minutes later.

"Hey, Max. Hope you don't mind if I move you." Those words filled Max with unbelievable desolation. Why? Did Tyler not like him anymore?

Tears fell down Max's face, soaking his chest as they dripped from his chin. It was a wonder the canvas didn't start leaking. Briefly he considered if that was the source of those paintings rumored to bleed or cry. Not a miracle, but some other poor schmuck trapped inside by a curse.

He didn't want to move away from Tyler.

Propped against the dresser, he couldn't see what Tyler was doing, but when Tyler hung him back up, facing Tyler with a better view than even from the head of the bed would be, he almost cried again from joy. He wanted to stay where he could watch over Tyler and listen to him. He only had the two senses left that received input from the outside world, and he wanted to fill them with Tyler.

CHAPTER FIVE

A shaft of sunlight, bright enough to irritate even through Tyler's closed lids, brought him to pain-spiked, eye-gouging wakefulness.

"Oh fuck. What was I thinking?" Tyler groaned and covered his eyes with a hand before allowing his lids to creep open. He really should have bought some fucking curtains already instead of drinking, although hopefully he wasn't going to be this stupid again. "Another hangover? It's like I'm in university all over again."

The sexy, naked man in his painting looked both self-righteous and amused. How did he do that?

"Yeah, yeah, Max, I'm an idiot. Don't rub it in. Trust me, I think I've wallowed in enough drunkenness for quite some time."

Tyler covered his eyes completely with a palm and rested the other gently on his roiling belly. What had he been thinking? This wasn't like him. Not at all.

Groaning again, he levered out of bed, wondering if he could eat a bit to buffer the painkiller he wanted to take. Stiffly, he made his way to the kitchen. Water didn't have any appeal this morning, but hydrating would help his hangover as much as anything else so he grabbed a bottle.

After the first few sips went down and stayed down—although there'd been some uncertainty on the subject—he rummaged in his cupboards. Finally, he laid hands on an old box of crackers. That would do until he could handle eating something else. Not that he had a lot of choices. Soy sauce, vinegar, olive oil, and spices seemed to be the sum total of his food-related items. There was a box of stale toaster pastries too, but the thought of their sugary icing made his stomach threaten to return the water. He'd relied far too much on take out since he'd moved.

Crackers and water in hand, he shuffled back into his bedroom. He tossed them on the bed and stepped gingerly into the bathroom, wondering if the presence of the toilet was going to trigger any fireworks. When nothing happened, he took a piss, grabbed a couple of painkillers, and returned to the bed to tuck himself back into his haven.

"Were you ever this stupid, Max?" Tyler nibbled on crackers between words. "Did you get drunk ever? Or take drugs? Artists sometime go for the mind-altering substances. Or could you not afford any of that?"

Tyler leaned back against his headboard, taking in every detail—again—of Max's beautiful form. He dozed off and on as the water and painkillers did their work. A few hours later, he roused, achy and uncomfortable, but more himself. This time, his gaze fell upon the box his sister had brought him yesterday.

He sat up, a trifle faster than was wise, but aside from a disgruntled throb in his temple, he didn't suffer a relapse.

"How did I forget about your box?"

As he hopped out of bed, Ty scratched his chest. And yelped. "What the fuck?"

Glancing down at his chest, he felt vaguely mortified he'd slept in the same shirt he'd gone to the club in. He must have been out of it, since he hated sleeping in shirts. At some point during the night, he'd exchanged his tight pants for a pair of boxers but failed to remove his shirt. Odd. Unbuttoning the shirt, he glanced around for a T-shirt he could replace it with.

"Oh God, Max. I was way too drunk last night. Look at this!" Ty pointed to the nipple rings that he'd somehow thought were part of a dream. If the nipple rings were real, then his memories of almost fucking Darren were probably real too. He was never drinking that much again.

Ty moved to his mirror. "Look pretty good, though, don't they? I wouldn't ever have done it sober, but I think I'll keep them." He'd have to ask Darren if there were any special instructions, because he didn't recall. Then he caught sight of his face. He looked like a goddamn raccoon.

With one last look at the box, Tyler stifled his excitement and headed to the bathroom. Shower first, then he could spend all day researching his new favorite subject.

Max groaned. Drunk Tyler had been adorable, at least when he didn't have some other man's tongue down his throat. He'd woken in the middle of the night to remove his pants, unfortunately replacing them with boxers. Then he'd stumbled about, muttering, and called his sister to inform her he'd taken her advice and gone out. When she finally understood what he was saying—and it was a slurred mess of sibilants—Max gathered she'd not been amused. Max enjoyed it, though.

But morning-after Tyler—rumpled, eyeliner smeared, and complete with matching nipple rings? Absolutely devastating. The weird mental arousal he experienced with Tyler ratcheted up, making Max wish with all his heart that Tyler would do whatever he had the other night to bring Max relief. Those little nipples were red, swollen, and standing at attention; aftereffects from the piercing. But Max suspected his mouth would have the same effect, given time and opportunity.

Clean, alert, and ready to work, Ty finally took note of two things. One, an unused condom packet on the floor—evidence of last night's embarrassment. Two, Max's new position on the wall—further evidence of Ty's complete drunken stupidity. Shit. Moving Max's painting in the middle of the night? He might have killed himself. Or broken a bone. It was a miracle he'd escaped without even a bruise. Or damaging his spectacular painting.

Unexplained, overblown terror swept through Ty, and he dashed to the painting. Once again, he carefully inspected both canvas and frame, this time searching for tears or breaks instead of illusions.

"I didn't hurt you or anything, did I?" Ty hoped he hadn't done something irreparable to Max. After several minutes his heartbeat returned to normal, and he relaxed. No damage was evident; he must have been lucky last night. Yet another reason not to drink so much.

Rising from his crouch, Ty grimaced. His muscles were still sore, but he didn't know if that was from moving Max or the lingering remnants of his hangover. As he turned, his heart rate elevated yet again. Time to open the box.

The grimy box sat on his desk, beckoning, and Ty yielded to the siren call. He smoothed his hands along the sides before tugging at the tattered tape whose glue had long since lost its tackiness. Flipping open the lid let out a billow of musty scent.

Ty peeled away the yellowed, fragile tissue, exposing a neatly folded but threadbare blue shirt. It was surprisingly unstained, given its decrepitude. Gingerly, he removed it from the box and placed it on the desk. Another work shirt lay underneath, in slightly better condition.

Curiosity got the better of his scholarly training for dealing with historical artifacts. Ty walked over to Max and held up the shirt to the strong, golden torso.

"Be a shame to cover you up, but this looks like it would fit you."

Decades had imprinted folds on the cloth, and Ty was able to easily return the shirt to its folded state. It joined its companion on the desk, along with a pair of soft, patched pants. Past another layer, Tyler found paint-spattered overalls and a paint-slathered, apron-type garment. The items immediately brought to mind an image of Max, paintbrush in hand, soft sunlight lighting up both his blond hair and the blank white canvas in front of him. Ty glanced over his shoulder at Max.

"These are a lot of clothes for you to have left behind. I haven't seen anything to suggest you were wealthy in your own right and able to discard wearable clothing. Decidedly unthrifty, considering the economics of the times."

The next layer was a pair of brown shoes that had been repaired multiple times. Bizarre to think about—Ty never had a pair of shoes repaired. Holes, major scuffs, rips meant replacement, not repair. Going through Max's clothes was alarmingly intimate and a bit sad too. He pulled the shoes out of the box, and a wallet fell out.

Excitement clawed at his throat. With trembling fingers he drew out two singles and a two-dollar bill. No identification, dammit. He took a closer look at the money. They were dated 1935, of interest in their own right as part of the first series of banknotes ever produced by the Bank of Canada. Apparently Dr. Carscadden's requirement that every professor in the department teach Intro to Canadian History at least every few years hadn't been a complete waste of time.

When the slight interest in the cash faded, Ty slumped into his chair. He wanted to see those police reports even more now. With every article he pulled out of the box, he'd been less and less convinced Max had left Victor's estate of his own free will. Maybe, just maybe, Max would have left clothes and a pair of shoes, but actual cash? No. Not a chance.

As he pushed the box to the side, intending to take a closer look at the wallet, something shifted. Ripping out the rest of the tissue, he saw a leather-bound book at the bottom. Reverently, he pulled it out and undid the leather tie holding it closed.

Was it...?

Ty took a breath and held it as he opened the cover.

It was. A journal. Not just any journal—Max's journal, proclaimed by the small, cramped handwriting on the flyleaf. Blood thumped in Ty's ears. Max probably...well, he was definitely dead, but as far as Ty was concerned, whatever day these items had been packed away had more than likely been the day Max was killed.

But a journal. It was an odd experience, wanting to laugh and cry at the same time. Personal papers were some of the most valuable and coveted for any historian. The nature of Max's death didn't matter. Not like there was anyone left alive to arrest. But Ty wanted to know about the man who would pose for such a graphic painting, who could incite a wealthy, powerful man like Victor Cranston to kill, but who left almost no trace of his existence beyond the contents of this box and an explicit, arousing painting. Did Max somehow foresee his demise? Was that why the painting had an aura of sadness?

Although Max seemed less unhappy than when Ty first laid eyes on him. Ty wondered how much of that was a reflection of his own mood. Which made about as much sense as the conversations he held with Max.

"Max, I found your journal." Apparently the conversations weren't ending anytime soon. Tyler sat in the plush, oversized chair situated to provide a clear view of Max. There was no good reason for the room configuration, but at least he didn't have to explain his choices to anyone.

He wanted to peruse the journal a little before he started properly authenticating and transcribing it. Maybe no one besides himself would be interested in the contents, but he couldn't turn off his scholarly instincts.

Ty flipped through a couple of pages but stopped at the first sketch he got to. It was a portrait of sorts—an older couple, two girls, and a man, all of whom resembled Max. The likenesses in the journal convinced Ty that Max's image was true to life—his face, anyway.

There was no caption for the rough sketch. Tyler hoped reading the journal would give him some indication of who was in the picture. The love of the artist for these subjects was apparent in every stroke.

"Is this your family? They look nice." Tyler flicked the picture toward Max even though he felt stupid doing so. Quickly but carefully skimming the journal, Tyler came across several more sketches, many of them featuring the same people in the original sketch. A couple featured the women wearing wedding dresses, although the dresses were lacking in detail compared to how intricate the faces were. The last few pages of the journal were empty, and the date of the last entry preceded the date of Max's reported disappearance on November tenth, by only a few days. He'd get more accurate information from the police reports, but Craig hadn't brought him any yet.

His gaze flicked up to Max. Regret filled him as he came to the unavoidable conclusion that this beautiful man had been killed by someone who'd never had to pay for his crime.

Tyler sat back and read from the beginning, a small notepad by his side in case he wanted to jot anything down.

May 28, 1937

Today is the first day I've had spare pennies in my pocket since April 2. Some might call a journal a needless extravagance, but with a full belly and a roof over my head, it was the first thing I wanted.

I don't know how I survived the last winter. Even if I thought I could eke out an existence on the farm for another year, the bank would not allow it. After six months alone, surrounded by nothing more than snow, the echoing loneliness in the farmhouse was almost unbearable.

My family had been bustling, loud, rambunctious—laughter laced with friendly arguments and discussions—even after Karl returned from the Great War. It took years for him to return to the happy, laughing older brother I knew. When I was sixteen, influenza took Father during the big blizzard of 1923. Karl became the head of the house. Taking a wife and making a few babies in quick succession aided Karl enormously in his outlook.

Karl and Mother always spoiled me, since I was the baby—or so Lena and Freya teased me. The farm had been doing well. Karl was expanding, hiring new farmhands, and although Father had insisted I apprentice with a local carpenter, Karl had other ideas for me. He knew how much I loved drawing. The success of the farm allowed him to indulge me, and he enrolled me in school in Toronto. The first of our family to go to university. I was indifferent to the idea of school, but Karl promised that if I got good grades, he'd pay for me to attend the Ontario College of Art after graduating.

Karl learned the value of education during the war. He saw how the educated were more likely to become officers and less likely to be machine gun fodder. Off I went, becoming a university graduate and thereafter an art student. My life changed immeasurably in that time, as I discovered how different city life was from farm life. I enjoyed my time until the crash—Black Tuesday. It affected everything and I saw but never comprehended. Karl kept me from knowing how badly it had affected my family. I lived in blissful ignorance—partly because Karl hoped the economic decline would not last long and partly because he knew how much I loved my classes. I am ashamed to say I didn't notice the frugalities my family employed when I returned for the holidays. Fewer farmhands, more root vegetables, less meat. It's not that I was particularly wasteful while I was at school. At least that's not on my conscience. But while I was having the best time of my life, my family was going through hardship.

There was a freedom to life off the farm I'd never known possible. I learned why I hadn't been interested in finding a wife like other men I knew. In the city, I discovered others like me. Not easily, not often, and always secret, but until I left the farm, I hadn't even realized why I was different.

Then an outbreak of cholera swept through my hometown. My nieces were the first to go, followed shortly by my sister-in-law.

I returned home for the funerals, and Karl told me I wouldn't be able to return to the city. Karl had arranged a marriage for me, to the daughter of one of the wealthiest women in the region. I hardly had time to process that, because he succumbed to cholera himself within days. My sisters' husbands were farmhands. Karl had allowed Lena and Freya love matches, but their husbands brought no financial support to the farm. Then my brothers-in-law, too, died, leaving me in charge of a family farm and three devastated women.

I'm ashamed to say I used the deaths as a way to indefinitely postpone my marriage. I had no idea, truly, what was needed to make a farm prosper. We limped along for a few years, my affianced bride married off to a better prospect, but we kept going. Until my sisters died in an accident and my mother wasted away from grief shortly thereafter.

Then it was only me. Six months I lived in the empty farmhouse, selling livestock and memories off as I could, watching crops wither and die in the fields. The bank harassed me regularly, but I kept clinging, kept struggling. I had no desire to ride the rails looking countrywide for a job that hundreds of others were competing for.

On the second day of April, almost two months ago, I walked into town to beg the bank for yet another extension on the mortgage. Without horse or automobile, it took three hours there and three hours back. When I returned to find the house in flames, I simply turned and walked away.

There was nothing left of my family's legacy and probably never would be. Without a farm, the pressing need for an heir subsided. There seemed no point in courting women I had no desire to bed or support. All I could see was my descent into starvation and degradation.

The droplet splashing onto the page was the first realization Ty had that he was crying. He quickly closed the journal and wiped at his eyes.

"Oh, Max. I had no idea. My grandmother told us stories, but I can't imagine how awful it would have been for you."

This was a first for Ty. He'd always felt a strong connection to the past, and he had a great capacity to empathize with the dead through the personal effects they left behind. It made him a good teacher and historian. But he'd never been moved like this before. Somehow the words in Max's journal made him as real as anyone Ty had ever met.

"You know what's funny?" Ty tried desperately not to imagine losing Mandy and Jake and his parents to untimely death. Along with losing his job, his means to support himself, his apartment. God.

"I was thinking, for a second, that I don't know anyone who writes in a journal. I was thinking how different the culture has become in less than a hundred years. But it's actually not true."

Grabbing his laptop, Ty tapped a few keys.

"See this?" He tilted a web page toward Max. "It's a blog. Stands for web log. I...well, explaining the web seems pointless, but this is a journal of sorts. There's also a phenomenon called social media. Places online where people can socialize, keep up with each other's lives. Almost like letter writing, except more spontaneous and with a lot more spelling errors."

Ty turned the laptop back to him and pressed a few more keys. "This is Facebook. It's like several people's interconnected journals. These are very similar to your journal—if you decided to publicize it and distribute it to everyone you know. Or read it aloud on a street corner for strangers' delectation." A stranger like him, who'd found Max by a string of coincidences.

Ty thought of many journals he'd transcribed and translated, all older than this. The comparison was quite apt.

"You'd be horrified by that idea, I bet. Most journals I've read for work were very personal, often containing very private thoughts. I'm not sure what it says about our society, where everyone puts their every little idea out there in public. Still, journal writing is more universal than I realized. Huh."

Wasn't exactly Ty's field, but maybe he could write a paper on it. It would allow him to keep Max's journal without feeling guilty for not turning it over to the university.

Max yearned to wipe the tears off Tyler's face. He'd never had anyone cry for him before, and as sweet as Max thought it was, he didn't want Tyler to be sad. Ever. Max pressed up against the glassy plane of his prison, then jumped back. With hands that weren't real, he pushed with both palms, and it bowed outward. The canvas seemed too thin under his touch, but Tyler gave no sign of noticing anything amiss. Harder and harder Max pushed, until it seemed his entire body passed the fixed point of his frame. So close—and yet not any closer at all.

Despair swamped him, obsidian shards slicing at his soul, and his own tears wet his face as he imagined curling into a ball on the ground. Was this what Victor had hoped would happen? Was this vicious tease the result of only meeting half the conditions of the curse? If so, Max might truly go mad.

He took a deep breath. He'd been strong enough to survive the loss of his family and exist for decades as a prisoner and unwilling voyeur; he could endure this. Wiping his face, he watched Tyler, focusing on his voice.

If all he could have was Tyler talking to him like he knew Max was there, well, that would have to do. Too bad he couldn't let Tyler know what topics he'd like to hear more about. Professors loved to lecture. Facebook? Blogs? Newspaper archives? Max wanted to hear more about them. They wouldn't tug painfully at his heart like Tyler's tears had. Max had been relieved Tyler hadn't cried or drunk more after Darren left. That told Max that Darren had been a convenience, nothing more. But if Tyler wasn't going to strip and masturbate for him, Max wanted to know more about the computer.

When he wasn't imagining licking Tyler from head to toe, nothing fascinated him as much as the computer did—in Tyler's hands, anyway. Why had Victor not used them to their full capacity? The things Tyler could do in mere moments without leaving his bedroom were amazing. And Max hadn't seen him pull up any porn yet, aside from the offhand comment about dick pics.

"Max, I'm feeling a little overemotional here. I'm hoping it's some strange side effect of the hangover." Ty smiled ruefully at Max. Maybe reading the journal right now wasn't a good idea. The tears threatened to bring his hangover headache back.

The phone rang, and Ty scrambled to answer, realizing he'd been stupidly staring at Max for the past several minutes.

"Hey, Mandy, what's up?"

"How are you feeling? Shitty, I hope." Although her tone wasn't vicious, she was pissed about something.

"I'm hungover. Why?"

"I know you're hungover, idiot. You called me last night, super drunk. Interrupted some of Jake's best work."

"I didn't call you last night. Did I?"

"Check your call log. I swear, just as Jake was --"

"Ah! Stop!" Ty's pickled brain put sense to Mandy's words—she'd meant Jake's best work in bed. And if Mandy never spoke again about her sex life with Jake, it would be too soon for Ty. "Did you call me just to torment me?"

"Why, didn't get any last night?"

Ty gritted his teeth. "None of your business."

"So, no, then?"

"Okay, I'm sorry I called last night. I'm hanging up now."

"No, wait, just want to confirm you're coming over on Wednesday for dinner."

"Ugh, Mandy, I'm not really in the mood." Last year he'd had a boyfriend to celebrate his birthday with. Last year, he knew his parents would at least call him for his birthday. This year, he wasn't so sure. "I don't really feel like celebrating. Can't I just stay twenty-nine for another year or twelve like any self-respecting gay man?"

"You're not spending your birthday alone. You can spend it with me, Jake, and Craig, or am I going to have to set you up?"

Ty shuddered. He hadn't forgotten his fear that Mandy was ready to buy him a prostitute. Even if she was talking blind date, spending his birthday by himself was a million times better than spending it making awkward small talk with a stranger. Mandy, Jake, and Craig were infinitely preferable to either of those depressing, soul-sucking options.

Having finally roused himself to hit the grocery store a couple hours ago, Ty finally had something besides prepackaged pastries to eat, and he prepared a simple dinner of steak and baked potato. Now that the hangover was limited to an ache in his joints, he was starving.

Mindful of the many comments he'd had on his social life recently, Ty also hooked up his television while his dinner cooked. Television was a rather solitary activity, but he knew Craig at least thought he was clearly having issues by not rushing to hook it up. While he ate, he watched it, but he couldn't stop looking at the bedroom door.

As soon as he'd finished eating and washing his dishes, he paced, knowing the restlessness derived from wanting to sit in the bedroom with Max, reading the man's journal. There wasn't any good reason not to, either, except for the fact that he might be giving his sister and friends a reason to worry. Hell, he was starting to worry himself, a bit.

His phone rang, interrupting his internal deliberations. Checking the caller ID, he saw it was Wendy. She was a lot of fun to hang out with, but if she was calling at eight on a Saturday night, she wanted him to go to a club with her. Once per weekend—that was all he could stand right now, especially since the aftereffects of his indulgence last night lingered. He silenced the ring. He wasn't up to defending his decision to stay home tonight to anyone, not even Wendy. Besides she'd probably just harass him about setting a date for a housewarming party, and he wasn't ready to cave on that yet.

Fuck it. He strode into the bedroom.

"Okay, Max, since there's nothing on television, I think it's a good night for reading in bed." Not Max's journal, though, no matter how much he wanted. There was no one here to witness his restraint, but he needed to prove to himself that he wasn't obsessed. And he didn't feel he needed to justify his decision to read in the same room as Max. He had an awesome comfy chair in his bedroom just perfect for reading; much more comfortable than the new couch he hadn't broken in yet. Right?

"What should I read?" He might not have done much unpacking but all of his mystery books had made it to his bookshelves. Mountains of boxes of reference books remained in the spare room that needed unpacking, but there was no rush for that.

Ty trailed his fingers along the spines, all displaying creases and cracks—evidence of how well loved they were. He paused by a few modern gay mysteries, but he wasn't sure he wanted to read anything with a romantic subplot, especially not with men. Too damn painful. Instead, he grabbed one of his favorites by Agatha Christie, *Murder in Mesopotamia.* He quickly read the copyright notice.

"This one was published in 1936, Max. Even if you read Agatha Christie, maybe you won't have read this one."

Snuggling with an afghan into his big comfy chair, Ty began to read. Aloud. And refused to consider why he was reading a book to a painting. Except for the fact that he didn't feel lonely when he included Max in his life.

CHAPTER SIX

Ty sat back in his seat. He should be stuffed—Mandy had put on a perfect spread for his birthday dinner—but with each hour that passed, his stomach knotted more and more. Picking at dinner had been the best he'd been able to do. During the day, he'd had the distraction of work, but it was becoming obvious that his parents weren't planning to call him for his birthday. He'd stopped by his apartment after work, pretending that he needed to change, and not that he wanted to check the mail for a card which didn't materialize.

At least Jake and Craig ate like horses on the edge of starvation, so he didn't need to worry about the food going to waste. It had been awhile since he'd seen the three of them, and there was a great deal of catching up to do, including rehashing the whole Jeffery incident.

Mandy brought out a birthday cake, complete with candles. Ty smiled half-heartedly as the three sang badly, then he made a wish and blew out the candles.

"Hey, Ty." Jake handed him a plate overflowing with cake and ice cream. "Mandy tells me she got you some historical porn. How's that working out for you?"

Ty coughed and blushed. He was almost certain that Jake wasn't asking how erotic Ty found it, but since it was his new favorite subject, he was happy to talk about the non-embarrassing aspects of Max. Suddenly ravenous, he started eating cake while he told them about the research he'd done so far, and what he hoped to accomplish when he had a chance to visit the county archives.

"By the way, that reminds me. Craig, did you have any luck finding those police reports?"

Jake sat up straighter, gaze intent on Tyler. "Police reports? Did you actually file a complaint against Jeffery?"

Craig rolled his eyes. "No, no. I was supposed to see if I can find the reports on ole' foot long's disappearance."

"Foot long?" Jake's eyes widened. "He's not really got a twelve inch cock, does he?"

The comments on Max's endowment flustered Ty enormously. "Shut up. It's not twelve inches, for God's sake. He was an artist not a porn star."

Jake just lifted a brow while Mandy and Craig laughed at him.

"Measured it, did you, baby bro?" Mandy asked with a giggle.

"No. You guys suck." His cheeks heated even more when he realized what he'd said, but at least they just laughed harder rather than poking any more fun.

When everything quieted down again, Jake spoke, saving Ty from having to keep harping on the same subject. "Were you able to find the old reports?"

Craig shook his head. "Not yet." He waved at the sling Jake still sported on his injured arm. "If some slackers would get back to work, I might have a few spare minutes to go on a wild goose chase."

"Oh. Whenever you can." Ty certainly understood. They might be heading into another long weekend for the August civic holiday, but Ty would be swamped trying to prepare for the end of the summer term. Only two and a half weeks left and he wasn't even close to having everything done. Max was an indulgence he didn't have time for but one he found far more interesting than grading essays and test papers.

"I haven't forgotten, but it seriously might not happen until Jake's back."

"Thanks, I appreciate that." Ty took another quick peek at his phone. There were two more birthday messages from friends, but none from his parents, nor a missed call. He swallowed heavily.

When he looked up, Mandy gave him a sympathetic look.

"On a related note, Ty, you want to come work at the shop this weekend? I'm really behind cataloging all of the shit from the Cranston estate and I could use a hand, especially since half my staff is heading up to cottage country for the long weekend."

Ty grimaced. Although there was the temptation of poking around to see if there was anything else of Max's, it seemed unlikely, since he already had the box of Max's possessions.

"Mandy, I don't know if I can. The move really set me back. I'm still playing catch up." He wasn't even lying. He'd helped his sister on many occasions, finding more interest in the items of other people's lives than most people would.

"You sure? I came across some unattributed, unsigned stuff. Possibly student work or practice work. No guarantees, but some of them are old—old enough to be Friedland's. I can let you spend some time with them, if you'll give me hand."

Ty frowned exaggeratedly, even though inside he was bouncing up and down with excitement. "Are you seriously blackmailing me? At a table with two cops? Rather brazen of you."

Jake snorted and Craig laughed as he grabbed another piece of cake.

Mandy flipped him her middle finger. "Hey, I gotta get my free labor somehow."

However true that was, she also knew how fascinated Ty had become with Max and the mystery of his disappearance. Always looking out for him, his big sis was. Well, what was a few more days behind? He'd manage to get the grades in on time somehow. He always did.

"Fine. But I can't work the whole weekend."

"Two days? Please?"

Ty sighed. "Okay. Two days."

Mandy clapped. "Awesome. You guys want to watch a movie or something?"

With another glance at his phone, which showed no new message from his parents, Ty's mood plummeted again. "Sorry I'm not in the mood, Mandy. And I've got early office hours tomorrow."

He expected Mandy to protest, but instead she just packaged up some more cake and put it with his birthday gifts while he hugged Jake and Craig.

Mandy walked him to the door and leaned in to kiss his cheek. Then she spoke quietly in his ear. "I know it's been hard for you. Mom and Dad suck; they really do. But they'll come around. Eventually. In the meantime, you've got me and Craig and Jake."

Moisture gathered in his eyes, and he hoped he wasn't going to cry. "I know. Thanks."

"You need anything, you call me. You hear?"

"Got it, sis."

Mandy gave him a hug that he wasn't able to properly return, his arms laden with gifts and cake. "See you Saturday, bright and early."

"I'm back, Max," Tyler announced as he walked into the bedroom.

Even a few feet away, Max saw the glitter of unshed tears. That wasn't right. Not on Tyler's birthday.

Abruptly, Tyler turned away and left the room. He returned with a bottle and a glass filled with ice. No beer today—Tyler was hell-bent on oblivion.

Tucked in the chair across from Max, Tyler drank two mouthfuls in silence before he started talking again.

"Max, you make a great roommate, you know? No judgment. No recriminations. No pressure to go out and get laid. Go out and find another boyfriend. Or even worse, go out and become heterosexual."

Tyler left his glass perched precariously on the edge of the desk as he picked up his phone and stared at it for a few moments.

"Parents are supposed to love you unconditionally, right?"

Max wasn't sure where this was going, but he wished he could provide more comfort than a captive audience.

"As soon as I told my parents I was gay, they said some vicious things and then stopped talking to me altogether. Cut me off completely."

Oh. Max's family might have done the same thing. His family wouldn't have wanted to know Max liked men—a surefire way to become the black sheep, the one talked about in hushed tones. He'd never have told them. But this was a different age, and Tyler apparently had other expectations.

"I know it's better that they know. I didn't like living a lie, but shit, it was hard. Mandy thinks I did it on purpose, you know. Chose exactly the wrong time, not giving them a chance to ease into the idea. Maybe she's right. I wasn't thinking clearly." Another mouthful of something slid down Tyler's eminently kissable throat, but Max couldn't read the label from this distance.

Max wasn't surprised Tyler had problems with the deception inherent in pretending to be straight. Besides being genuine, he couldn't lie for shit. Max wanted to know more about him, and this source of pain would hopefully lighten if he talked about it—before he devolved into incomprehensible drunken muttering.

"I don't think Jake would approve of me drinking my birthday gift like this, but fuck it. My parents truly have cut me off. They didn't call or send a card for my birthday. So that's it."

Ty poured another two fingers into the glass and stared into the amber depths.

"Of course, I'd already broken up with Preston, but I realized I was ready to bring a boyfriend home with me. Ready to have a partner be a part of the family. There didn't seem to be any good reason to keep hiding from my parents. They needed to know the truth, and I was finally ready to tell them. At Christmas dinner, I dropped the big old 'I'm gay' bomb."

The scent of a perfectly cooked turkey usually made Ty's mouth water, but he'd suffered from low-grade nausea ever since breaking up with that cheating, lying skunk three weeks ago.

"You need to eat something," Mandy whispered. A worry line creased her forehead, and he tried to smile at her and Jake.

"I will," he whispered back. Maybe. Last Christmas dinner hadn't been like this. Sure, he and Preston had spent it apart, but they'd only recently started their relationship. The empty sixth chair hadn't taunted him like it was going to this year.

Ty loved Jake almost as much as Craig. Jake was a good fit for his sister, but sitting at the table with his parents, sister, and brother-in-law only emphasized that he'd always be the fifth wheel. His gift to Preston—a key to his apartment—had been carefully wrapped over a month ago and still lay under his tree at home. Mistaking the depth of their relationship, Ty had intended to ask Preston to move in—a big step for someone whose parents didn't know he was gay.

"Tyler, dear, eat something." His mother echoed Mandy's statement and tapped a perfectly manicured nail on the rim of her wineglass. "You need to find a wife to look after you."

Ty started to make the noncommittal noises he always made when his parents mentioned him getting a woman. Then he stopped abruptly and shook his head. It was time. Preston wasn't "the one", but Ty would find him someday, and if he wanted "the one" to sit at this table with his sister and her husband, he needed to tell them the truth. Hell, he could get married too, if he found the right partner, and he didn't want that to be a secret. But he'd need to make that final step. Smash the damn closet to pieces.

"Mom, Dad, I have something to tell you."

Mandy gasped and widened her eyes. Jake nodded in encouragement. Ty's announcement wasn't going to be a surprise to either of *them*.

His mother's eyes shone in the candlelight, expectant. His father gave him as much attention as he ever did. They weren't expecting him to announce he had a wife in mind, were they? No. They must suspect something. He'd never brought a girl, or anyone else, home.

Ty sucked in a breath. "I'm gay." The air escaped in a relieved rush. Quick, scary, painful, but done and over. He'd said it; it was out there. Like ripping off a bandage.

Mandy smiled, but his parents stared at him as though he were a stranger.

"You're not gay." His father gave the last word an unpleasant twist. It was the first thing he'd said since they sat down, besides "Pass the potatoes."

"That's not funny, dear," his mother said. To him, not his father.

"I am." Well, coming out probably wasn't easy for anyone. Mandy patted his hand.

"There's only one girl in this family. That's your sister." His father returned his attention to his meal, ignorant of the bands of despair tightening around Ty's body, making him light-headed and faint.

"Being gay doesn't mean I'm a girl!"

"This is unacceptable, Tyler Williams." Oh, his mother had been paying attention to him. "And for God's sake, don't joke like this with anyone else. Someone might believe you. How embarrassing."

"Embarrassing? It's not a joke, Mom. I like guys. And I want what Mandy has. I want to bring my husband to dinner with my family."

His mother let out a horrified shriek. "You didn't get married, did you? To a man?"

"No, but someday I might." He would. They couldn't all be like Preston.

"I won't have it. I won't have any perverts at my table. And if you don't stop talking about it, you can leave."

"Mother, don't say that." Mandy to his rescue, since he wasn't sure he was still breathing.

"Dad?" His voice cracked, and his eyes burned.

His father wouldn't look at him, but his fork was held tightly enough that his knuckles whitened. "Listen to your mother."

Listen to his mother? His mother thought he was a pervert. He'd have to find more than a bandage now that his parents had decided to cut him to ribbons.

But his father wasn't done. "Who else can carry on the family name? No son of mine is a fairy. I'd never be able to hold my head up at work. Or the club."

Where was all this coming from? His parents had never hinted they were bigoted. Not once.

Ty stood, shaking, and jabbed his fingers against the table as he spelled out his points. Each muffled thump was accompanied by a rattle of dishes. "Carry on the family name? It's Williams! There are millions of us out there. And I'm sure you've got coworkers who are gay, not just ones who have gay kids."

His father gave a dismissive grunt. "If that's true, they've had the decency to keep quiet about it."

Decency?

Jake wasn't standing, but he transformed before Ty into a wary cop, alert for danger.

Ty wasn't in danger of doing anything except tossing his cookies or crying like the girl his father thought he was.

"Fine. I'm leaving." His voice only wobbled a bit, but he could forgive that of himself.

"Stop this nonsense, and eat your dinner, Tyler." His mother spoke as though they hadn't toppled Ty's self-worth like a demolished building.

In his scramble to leave the table, his chair overturned, but he kept going, grabbed his coat and shoes, and stumbled out into the snowy driveway without putting either on.

His fingers shook, and it took him a few seconds to unlock and open the car door. He managed to throw the coat and shoes inside before he fell to his knees, heaving up what little he'd eaten into the rhododendron bushes lining the drive.

A hand rubbed his back gently, heavier and warmer than Mandy's.

Finally the heaves subsided.

"You okay?" Jake asked. Ty crawled away and stuffed a handful of fresh snow into his mouth. Jake hauled him up and dragged him around the car to place him in the passenger seat. Shaking his head, he wrapped Ty in his coat before dusting off his socks and shoving his feet into his shoes. Jake would make a great father someday.

"Where's Mandy?"

"Talking some sense into your parents. Or trying to."

Jake belted him in before he moved to the driver's side and started the car. "Let's get you home."

"But Mandy... I can drive."

"Ty, even if you weren't my friend and brother-in-law, I'm a cop. No way am I letting you drive like this. Mandy's got keys for our car; she'll make her own way home."

"I'm sorry." Hot air began blasting from the heaters, but Ty was frozen from the heart out.

"You don't have anything to be sorry for."

Nice of Jake to say, and if he weren't freezing to death, he'd be blushing over his emotional reaction. "But I --"

"Look, you've been through a lot the past couple of weeks. Your reaction is totally understandable." Jake pulled into the garage for his and Mandy's condo.

"Why are we here?"

"You're not staying at home alone. Not today."

"I'm not going to do anything stupid." A natural assumption for a cop, but Ty wasn't suicidal.

"I know that. But your sister would kick my ass if I left you on your own after this."

"I ruined your dinner. You must be starving."

Jake laughed. "I'm a cop, remember? Half of my Christmas dinners have been Chinese food. Don't worry about me. Once we get you settled, I'll call in an order."

A small giggle escaped. Despite the hateful words and unfortunate stomach rebellion, Chinese food with his sister and brother-in-law didn't sound half bad. May be the best Christmas dinner he'd ever had.

Tears tracked down Tyler's face. Max sniffled too. Ty was an excellent storyteller, which would be an invaluable skill for a history professor.

Tyler rubbed his eyes and drank a little more. "It's well into the twenty-first century, and I thought my parents were enlightened people. But they weren't. I don't know what's going to happen this Christmas."

He sucked back the rest of the booze in one gulp and flung the glass across the room. Max expected it to shatter, but it just made a dull thud against the wall as it bounced, then rolled to a stop.

"Stupid plastic glasses," Tyler muttered. "Still, I'd better stop or I'm going to be completely useless at work tomorrow."

Tyler should be grateful he was drinking out of a plastic glass. Cleaning the mess from that sort of temper tantrum was never worth the momentary satisfaction of breaking glass.

Stroking the walls of his prison as he would Tyler's cheek, Max wished he could hug Ty, kiss away the tears and the adorable pout. Tyler crawled into his bed, still muttering in disgruntlement as he pulled the covers over himself and curled into a ball. When the tipsy snores started, Max contented himself with absorbing every detail of the sleeping man. Beautiful, adorable, sexy man. What Max wouldn't give to wrap his body around Tyler, make him forget his shithead boyfriend and his disapproving parents.

CHAPTER SEVEN

Max watched Tyler all night—so beautiful, so sweet. He'd spent the last two evenings recovering from his ill-advised mid-week birthday binge, and had continued reading more Agatha Christie novels to him. Max had very much enjoyed being read to, although Tyler had fallen asleep right before he revealed who the murderer was. Hopefully, Tyler would finish reading the book to him soon; thinking about the possible clues kept Max's brain whirling all night. Although he appreciated a book from his era, he wouldn't take it amiss if Tyler would read something a little more modern. Max was interested to find out if literature had changed as much as technology.

Tyler woke finally, looking about as well rested and stress free as Max had ever seen him.

With his arms stretched above him, the sweatpants slipped down a bit, drawing Max's gaze to his morning wood. Tyler smiled at him.

"Morning, Max." He sauntered off to the bathroom and returned quickly enough that he couldn't have done more than piss. Which Max was grateful for. If the man was going to masturbate, he wanted to watch.

Tyler touched his journal again, and Max sensed the yearning. Why, he wasn't quite sure. Max didn't recall with any clarity what he'd written, beyond some specific memories of his family and his very short time with Victor, but he didn't know why even a history professor would care about him and his thoughts. Tyler did, though; that much was obvious, as well as how torn he was about caring.

Instead of opening the journal, as Max expected, Tyler flipped open his laptop and began typing. From Max's new vantage point, instead of Tyler's back, he saw Tyler's profile and the adorable expression of concentration focused on the screen.

After much typing and note-taking, Tyler sat back and sighed.

"Hey, Max." Max was never going to tire of how completely Tyler included him in his activities. "I think I've got enough information now to hit the county records office, although it might have to wait until my break between summer session and fall term. Get some information on your family and the location of your farm. There is a lot of farmland left in the Kitchener/Waterloo area, so it would be cool to know if your family's farm still exists."

Max would think it "cool" too. But what did it matter to him? The bank had probably sold the land to the highest bidder—Max had no heirs or other family that he knew of. Another Friedland would never again till its soil.

"Of course, I don't expect to learn much about you, since according to your journal, I wouldn't even be able to see the house you lived in. The trip will satisfy some curiosity, but it won't tell me about you, specifically."

Max understood. He might not know why Tyler had taken him on as a project, but it was clear he'd taken on Max, the man, not Max, some random murder victim from the Great Depression.

With a satisfied little smile, Tyler settled into the chair that looked vastly more comfortable than the one he'd used while on the computer, and opened Max's journal.

June 1, 1937

In desperation, I returned to the familiar—the art school in Toronto. I tracked down my old mentor, Arthur. For a time after I'd been forced to return home, I'd remained in correspondence with him, but eventually it became too painful as I reconciled myself to living the life of a farmer.

I'd found a rooming house and began doing whatever odd jobs I could find. I thought perhaps my old mentor might have some artistic-related work for me. Or I hoped he did. If nothing else, maybe the city would have more opportunities for work than the country.

It was Arthur who told me about Victor. Between Victor's unrepentant love for men and his great wealth, the public was unsure how to treat him. Victor was accepted by society—mostly—but was snickered at and held in some contempt by those who didn't pretend he was invisible. I was desperate, and although we never spoke of such matters, I believe Arthur suspected I had similar proclivities and wouldn't object to such a sponsor.

I began a correspondence with Victor, via introductions from Arthur. Victor was anxious to sponsor a qualified candidate. Although I've never much understood exactly what a patron gets out of the arrangement, I wasn't about to deny the benefits I would reap. At least I'd have a roof over my head and food in my belly. I am grateful for Arthur's assistance. Midway through the month of May, Victor agreed to meet with me. A couple of days later, I was moved into a carriage house on Victor's property, a small stipend in my pocket, a safe place to lay my head, and unable to believe in my good fortune.

For the first few days, Victor was rarely at home. The butler, Stavers, ensured I had all the equipment I needed, as well as that I was settling in. The bed was lumpy. The food was sparse and cheap. But it was better than I'd had in months.

The equipment, though, made me quail. Victor had spared no expense. It was the first time I realized just how high his expectations were, and it had been years since I'd picked up a paintbrush.

Terrified, I pleaded with Stavers to get some lower-quality stuff—practice canvases and less expensive paints. Fortunately, he complied.

June 13, 1937

Today was terrifying. Without supervision, I'd painted pictures from my heart, covering several canvases with portraits of my family from memory. I'd been amazed and pleased at how quickly all my skills came back, as though merely dormant, rather than excised from my soul, as I'd begun to imagine. When Victor appeared in the studio, he was furious, yelling and throwing things, like a cross between a spoiled little boy and a candidate for the sanitarium. Apparently I was supposed to be painting landscapes and wilderness scenes like the Group of Seven. Stavers had not seen fit to mention this, nor had Victor, but there was no sense in pointing fingers. All I could do was apologize and hope my sponsorship hadn't ended as abruptly as it had begun.

I quickly assured Victor I'd start painting what he desired immediately and still managed to save one painting from destruction. Obviously, I will have to keep that hidden from Victor in the future, else he destroy that one too.

Grant, the other occupant of the modified carriage house, is a talented, attractive young sculptor. I am ashamed to admit that, despite finding him as self-absorbed and shallow as our sponsor, the mere proximity of our rooms and the look in his eyes as he appraised Victor led me to believe we might enjoy some mutual satisfaction. I'm hesitant to speak freely, though, as I am still feeling my way and don't want to get kicked out if I've misread the situation.

Ty gasped and hugged the journal to his chest. Could this be in the group of paintings Mandy had found? He opened his mouth, wanting to tell Max, but was afraid to say it aloud in case it wasn't there, or there was no way to determine if it was Max's, or if the Cranston heirs, for whatever reason, refused to sell it to him. Tyler wanted something else Max had touched, something Max had loved. Only one way to find out.

"Well, that's it for now, Max. I promised Mandy I'd help her catalog some of the stuff from Victor's estate. I'll have to make notes on the pages I just read when I get home, otherwise I'll be late enough that Mandy will kick my ass."

Before dressing for what he expected to be dirty, grueling work, Ty looked up a few addresses on the laptop. He decided to walk to Mandy's gallery rather than take the subway. The fresh air would do him good. On the way, though, he could stop by a few Max-specific landmarks.

He was out the door and locking it behind him before he paused. Should he take the journal with him?

Ty returned to the bedroom and touched the journal on his desk. Bringing it with him might damage the journal, or he could lose it, both of which were hideous to imagine. But having the sketches inside might help him determine if any of the artwork was Max's. After a few more minutes of internal debate, he grabbed a pillowcase, painstakingly wrapped the journal, and stuck it in the messenger bag that usually housed papers he needed to grade. Slinging it over his shoulder, he waved at Max and left.

An hour and a half later, Ty arrived at Mandy's gallery.

"Where the hell have you been?"

Nowhere important. The renamed Ontario College of Art and Design looked nothing like what Max would have seen when he attended. He'd walked by Victor's estate also, but he could barely see the house from the gate. Most of the land had been turned into housing developments, but some was still parkland. Was Max's body buried close to the house? Or in those wooded areas? He had to assume Victor wouldn't allow construction to take place where a murder victim could be unearthed.

"Sorry. It was a longer walk than I expected."

Mandy pursed her lips, but Ty didn't see any reason to 'fess up about his detours.

"Whatever. Follow me."

His sister led him through the gallery to a room in the storage area. It wasn't large, but it was filled with canvases. She handed him a tablet.

"Holy crap, sis. When did you get all high-tech?"

"When I fired my last assistant and realized I couldn't read any of the forms he'd filled out. I needed to re-inventory half my stock. It's pretty simple. I've put catalog numbers on all of the paintings. Just enter the number, take a photo, and type in the measurements and description. It'll sync up with my database."

"Okay." When Mandy has said she'd wanted his help, Ty hadn't realized he could end up spending all day on artwork alone. He figured he'd also be cataloging a bunch of knick knacks and things destined for Something Old. Maybe that was tomorrow's task.

Mandy smiled and left him.

Hours later, Ty was completely discouraged. Why had Victor kept all this crap? Okay, to be fair, it wasn't all crap, but the majority of the landscapes weren't worthy of more than gracing a hotel room's walls, and moderate ones at that.

His depression originated from more than his offended aesthetic sensibilities, though. Ty had imagined he'd be able to touch a painting and magically know Max had painted it. But all the damn landscapes blurred and looked the same.

At least he only had a dozen or so more.

He grabbed a lake scene done in all shades of gray and moved it to his "done" stack. He turned to the next painting, and his breath caught in his throat.

Afraid he was dreaming, he reached out to touch the painting. It was real.

"Where the fuck is my bag?" Ty scrambled for the small desk beside the door, where he'd left his messenger bag. He pulled out the journal and flipped to the sketch of what he believed was Max's family. The similarities between the sketch and painting were undeniable and striking.

"Mandy!" Ty yelled. He didn't know where in the storage area she was, and he was worried if he took his eyes off the portrait, it would disappear.

His sister came in at a run. "What? What?"

"This one. This is Max's."

She threw up her arms. "Oh, for God's sake, Ty."

"Look at this." Ty shoved the sketch into her field of vision.

"Shit. This was in the box I brought you?" Mandy was almost as excited as Ty. He wasn't the only one who liked a good mystery.

"Yep. What do you think?"

Mandy sighed. "You want it, don't you?"

"Can you get it for me? I'll pay." Ty was nearly dancing.

Trailing her fingers across the sketch, Mandy smiled. "I'll get it for you. I'll get you a good price too. Unsigned—it's not worth a lot, and I'm sure the heirs will be glad to part with it. When I know, you'll know."

Ty hugged his sister.

"Jeez, if I'd known you were going to get all mushy, I'd have never got you that naked man picture in the first place."

"Yeah, yeah."

Working for Mandy was always more taxing than he expected but he could barely keep his attention on his work. He kept going back to check on "his" painting. How much was that painting going to set him back? He had some savings, and he knew Mandy would negotiate the best price. Was he a fool? Buying a painting of someone else's family... Was that a sane thing to do? Sane or not, he wanted it.

Three hours later, filthy and exhausted, Ty finished cataloging the paintings. After one last longing look at the only non-landscape in the bunch, he headed home. How many showers was he going to have to take in one day?

Max was truly impressed by Tyler's strength of will. There was no mistaking Tyler's desire to read and assess Max's journal—and he hardly remembered what he'd written in there—but after reading a few pages early Saturday morning, he'd focused on work, either his own or Mandy's. Of course, Tyler didn't just read the pages. That would have taken almost no time at all. For each page of journal, Tyler wrote reams of notes, and investigated anything Max mentioned, cross-referencing and verifying as best he could with the tools on his computer. It was fascinating and at the same time a little embarrassing. Max's life wasn't worthy of so much intense scrutiny. He'd never accomplished anything except for proving—to himself, if no one else—that the paranormal existed. There wouldn't be any kudos for that dubious achievement.

At night, Tyler decompressed and relaxed by reading to Max, something they both enjoyed, although Tyler couldn't know that either. They'd finished Death on the Nile last night, and Max had been waiting patiently for him to return from his day at the university to find out what they were going to read next.

Max's gaze drifted to the digital clock beside Tyler's bed. Normally, Tyler was home by now, unless he'd gone out after work. Unease curdled his midsection. Tyler hadn't mentioned dating or men recently, but that didn't mean he wasn't out on a date right now. No matter how much Max didn't want to share with another man, nor watch Tyler have sex with someone else in front of him, neither did he want Tyler to be unhappy. It wasn't hard to tell how much Tyler wanted a boyfriend and there was no real reason he should give up in his search. After all, Tyler was everything Max could want in a man—it stood to reason he'd be perfect for a man who wasn't trapped in a painting.

"Hey Max!" Tyler strode into the room carrying a bulging plastic bag and his messenger bag. He looked hot, sweaty, and disheveled, but that didn't stop Max from sighing in relief. Today, he wasn't going to have to worry about a boyfriend.

"It's crazy hot and humid out there, and office hours went forever. There's only two more weeks in the summer session, and everyone's freaking out about their grades. But I brought home Thai for dinner, and I'm going to take a break tonight, because it's going to be flat out crazy until after exams are done."

What did he bring home for dinner? Max didn't know what it was like outside Tyler's apartment, but takeout from a plethora of ethnicities was readily available.

Tyler changed quickly, and puttered for a bit before he sat at his desk to eat. Max was well aware that Tyler spent more time than he should in his bedroom, because of Max, but Max couldn't bring himself to be upset about it. He loved every second Tyler chose to be in his presence.

The food Tyler started eating had vegetables and noodles, but Max still didn't know what word he'd used to describe it.

With an inquiring tilt of his head, Ty chewed and stared at Max. When he'd finished that mouthful, Tyler spoke again. "Do you even know what Thai food is? It's from Thailand."

Thailand? Max was still lost. What he wouldn't give for access to Tyler's laptop—and a few lessons on how to use it.

Tyler laughed. "You know, this is actually pretty awesome. I'm usually so immersed in medieval history, I don't really pay attention to anything as modern as...well, you. But every time I say something to you, I wonder if it's something you would have known when you were alive or not. And now that I'm thinking about it, I don't remember when Thailand changed its name."

He ate a little more while he typed on his laptop, and it was several minutes before he looked at Max again.

"Okay, so you might have had Chinese food. Apparently there were a number of Chinese restaurants in Toronto while you were living. But Thai restaurants don't seem to be have become common until the late twentieth century."

Chinese. Yes, he'd had Chinese food a couple of times. A few of his university friends had introduced him to the cuisine and he'd adored it.

"Well, Thai food is similar to Chinese food, at least in my opinion. Maybe my palate is too unsophisticated." Ty laughed again. "But if you knew about Thailand the country, you'd have known it as Siam. It became Thailand in 1939, so after your time, if the journal and anecdotal evidence is anything to go by."

Max had learned so much from Tyler from these little snippets of lectures, almost as much as he'd learned over the years watching television with Victor. He had no idea why Tyler bothered, but it just made him care for Tyler more and more every day.

After dinner, Tyler cleaned up, took a quick shower, and pulled on the sweat pants that doubled as his pajamas. He remained shirtless, for which Max was grateful. He went to his mystery bookshelf and pulled out a book.

"I'm in the mood for something slightly different. A little more modern." Tyler winked at him before he settled in bed.

Tyler started reading, and the differences were immediately apparent. Curse words aplenty, with a grouchy main character who was brutally frank.

Max had just started to get lulled by the rhythm of the story, which was a quite different than Tyler's previous offerings. A little more graphic, a little more violent. Night fell, the bedside table lamp casting long shadows across the bed.

He listened raptly. The main character was gay. And unless Tyler was making fiction of his own, there was explicit sex on the page. Max wanted to grab the book and see for himself. He also wouldn't mind recreating the scene with Tyler.

When Tyler's voice got a bit breathy, Max knew they were both turned on. And just like that, the walls of his prison got stretchy. Max pushed and pushed, getting more turned on as Tyler did.

"Sorry, Max. I think I have to call it a night."

Tyler turned out the light and set the book aside. Max didn't know who the murderer was, but he didn't care. Tyler was putting on a different sort of show for him, one he had no intention of missing.

For many years, Max had never wanted anything more than oblivion, long superseding his yearning for freedom. But Max's desire for this man was stronger than either, and he longed for his freedom if only to touch the compelling, beautiful man in front of him.

CHAPTER EIGHT

"Max, do you know what today is?"

Thanks to a digital clock beside Tyler's bed that had quite a lot of information on it, including outside temperature, Max knew it was Saturday, but Tyler had never been quite this giddy about a Saturday before.

"It's the first day of my break! Another hour's work or so, and I'll have all my grades submitted, and then two and a half weeks of bliss."

Tyler laughed. "Okay, maybe not all bliss. I have to do some prep for the fall classes, but mostly I can concentrate on you and getting the rest of the apartment unpacked. Maybe pick a date for a housewarming party before Wendy blows a gasket. I think she's partly hoping it'll devolve into some sort of gay orgy she can watch, but she'll be disappointed."

True to his word, Tyler worked on his laptop for about an hour before he gave a triumphant shout, and closed the lid. He picked up Max's journal and the notebook where he'd made reams of notes and curled up in the plush chair across from Max.

The odd thing was, Tyler didn't read the journal entries aloud like he did with the mysteries, but he would occasionally comment on them. But Max didn't mind the silence, too much. As long as Tyler was in the room, he was happy.

July 28, 1937

I finally won over Stavers. His one indulgence is his rocking chair, and it broke today. I was able to fix it quickly and solidly, without Stavers having to hire out a carpenter. As I well know, there is no shortage of carpenters looking for work, but easy access has to count for something. He almost smiled when I offered carpentry services as needed around the estate.

August 7, 1937

Victor came to visit the studio again today. Same as always, he stood too close and touched me whenever and wherever he could. What can I do, though? After the rocking chair incident, Stavers is very good about interrupting. We're not friends, but more like combatants fighting a common enemy for different reasons. He senses my reluctance to give Victor what he wants, and I think he respects me for my resolve. But if it comes down to an ultimatum, I'm not sure what I'd choose, whether I could maintain my resolve. Arthur has put me, unbeknownst to him, in an almost untenable position between Victor, who wants me, and Grant, who wants Victor. At this point, I'm sure I want neither, but I also don't want to give up my admittedly cushy, yet creatively stifling, sponsorship.

August 16, 1937

I seem to have acquired a cat. I wouldn't dare ask Stavers for extra rations for a stray, despite his softening towards me, but every night for the past week, it's come to my window. I've saved small portions of my dinner, and it's nice having something I can care about again. Company that has no ulterior motives. The cat is small and orange and will allow me to scratch its head while it eats, but no more.

Ty took a deep breath as his heart swelled. Reading the journal made him want a cat too. He liked cats, and if he'd moved in with Preston, he'd been intending to suggest getting one. But he'd been reluctant to get one while he was single. That was a stereotype he didn't want to fill. But maybe he'd been wrong. Maybe, like Max said, it would be company, something to love unconditionally.

September 15, 1937

Last night was awful. Victor had a large dinner party for some of the wealthy elite in the art patronage circles. Grant and I were brought out and displayed like trained, talking monkeys. Of course, we were not allowed to eat with the rest of the guests. Maybe once we make a name for ourselves, we'd be welcome. That was fine with me, although Grant kicked up a bit of a fuss—with Stavers. When he spoke to Victor next, he was all sunshine and smiles. He knows as well as I do which side his bread's buttered on.

But that wasn't the awful part. For the first time, I saw married men, wealthier versions of the men I'd had sex with, in the same venue as their wives. It was easy to see which men had been with Victor and which ones were slated for conquest, by the interaction between them. Subtle, yes, but significant. Not that the entire party was full of queers like me, but I'd guess

Victor had invited a number of like-minded fellows.

Their wives, though, as much as they tried to hide it, each and every one showed their hurt, anger, shame. Which, in turn, shamed me. I'd imagined marriage would mean I'd never be with another man. Vows spoken before God should not be broken lightly. Which was why I'd put off my own marriage. But I'd never considered—fully—the effect the adultery had on the wives who endured their husbands' infidelity. Every one of those women hated Victor. And I realized I'd likely been the target of a lot of similar emotion.

I'm thirty now, and although I'd always been discreet and rarely indulged my baser desires, I vowed never to willingly participate in adultery again, no matter what my prick thought about it. I could have slaked my lust with any one of Victor's former lovers. They gave me enough signals to indicate their desire. But I couldn't do it to their wives. Between my reluctance to commit adultery and my qualms about having sex with either Victor or Grant, my prick is starting to despair.

Insistent and obnoxious buzzing startled Ty awake. Max's journal lay open, facedown, on his bare stomach, and he caught it as it began to slide to the floor. Shit. He knew better than to treat historical documents cavalierly, but he'd not been able to stop reading.

"Hold on. Jeez." Ty placed the journal on the desk and hoisted his sweatpants up. The buzzing stopped.

Wondering if the impatient visitor had given up or was only taking a rest, Ty wandered out into the living room. Heavy footfalls pounding up the stairs were quickly followed by an even more insistent banging on his door.

"Tyler!" Craig shouted. "Open this fucking door right now!"

Ty scrambled to obey. "What's wrong?"

Craig glared and pushed into his apartment. "I've been calling and buzzing for, like, ten minutes. I thought you were dead or something."

Craig's gaze traveled up and down. In any other man, Ty might have assumed he was being checked out, but Craig was inspecting him for damage.

"Nah. I was just asleep."

"Clearly you're not going to have time to look these over before we go." Slapping a file folder with one hand, Craig frowned. "You're showering, right?"

Sleeping during the day was never a good idea for Ty; it fogged his brain up. "Look over what? Why am I showering?"

Not answering, Craig looked around the apartment. "Oh for fuck's sake. What have you been up to? You've still hardly done anything around here."

Ty hadn't quite realized how much time he'd spent researching Max.

"Hey. I hooked up the television. This is the first day of my break, remember? It may not be taking down drug dealers or murderers, but I do work for a living. And I've been studying Max's journal. It's fascinating."

"I'm a little worried about you and how much time you're spending on Max, the penile wonder."

If he wasn't annoyed, he'd have laughed. "You do know that researching the past is actually my job, right? I've not even put a fraction of the time into Max that I did into researching my doctoral thesis. There's no need to worry."

Craig grunted, and Ty realized it was probably more of his lack of dating that was concerning Craig rather than Max. He wished people would just butt out of his love life. When he found a man as interesting and honorable as Max, then he'd consider dating him.

"There's not much in here, but now I'm glad we're not going to have time to go through them." Craig tapped the file folder he'd thrown on the table, and he relaxed onto the couch.

Curious, Ty plopped down beside him and reached for the folder.

"No." Craig smacked his hand.

"What the hell's in there?"

"The police reports you asked me to get."

Ooh. Awesome. He reached for the file again and got another smack for his trouble. "Hey!"

"No time. Get in the shower. You stink."

"Since when do you care?"

"I don't, but Mama will."

Mama? "Oh shit. Dinner tonight." Ty didn't want to skip out. He liked Craig's family, and the food was always great, but he didn't feel like going out again. He wanted to read the police reports. Maybe read more of the journal. There wasn't much left.

"Yes. And you're going. You promised at your birthday dinner—the first Saturday of your break. You can't disappoint my mama." Craig thrust out his chin, and Ty recognized his stubborn expression. If Craig had to pick him up and toss him in the shower, he would.

"Fine. I'm going." He managed not to stomp into the bathroom.

A glance in the mirror confirmed he looked a bit like a savage, hair sticking up randomly and a streak of dirt on his cheek. For some bizarre reason, he was embarrassed more for Max to see him this way than Craig. The notion was crazy enough to propel him into the shower to prepare for some real-world interactions.

Ten minutes later, Ty was out of the shower and pulling mostly clean clothes onto his still-damp body. He needed to get some laundry done.

"Well, Max, I wish I was staying home with you tonight. Craig brought over some old police reports. I'm quite interested to see if they offer any new information."

"Are you talking to that fucking painting?" Craig bellowed from the living room, and Ty's fingers slipped off the buttons he was trying to do up.

"Uh, no." Even Ty didn't believe he sounded convincing. Somehow it had become second nature for him to talk to Max, but anyone else would think it weird.

Craig burst into his room without a knock. "Aren't you dressed yet, crazy man?"

Ty relaxed. If Craig thought he was having a disastrous mental breakdown for real, he wouldn't have been brusque or used the word crazy.

"You moved the painting."

Oops. Ty had forgotten about that. Craig assessed the new position of the painting relative to the bed, and the brick red flush on Craig's cheeks told Ty exactly why Craig thought he'd moved the painting.

He wasn't entirely wrong, but his stroke-off material wasn't the sort of information Ty felt comfortable sharing with anyone, much less his very straight friend. And he couldn't admit to anyone that Max had become even more than "inspiration."

Craig shook his head. "Just hurry up, would you?" He slipped out of the room to let Ty finish dressing.

"Ha. Teach him to..." Ty glanced at Max, then the bedroom door. Maybe he should try to curtail the Max conversations. At least while Craig was here.

"Night, Max. See you later," Ty couldn't help whispering before he joined Craig.

"Tyler, honey!" Mama D'Amato pulled Ty's face down and kissed both cheeks. "I made your favorite tonight. Ziti. You know I would have cooked for your birthday, if you'd wanted."

"Thanks, Mama. Mandy wanted to do it, though." Craig's mom had always been sweet to him, but Ty noticed more now. Eyes burning with unexpected tears, he let himself be buffeted by Craig's dad, who gave him a big hug.

"Good to see you, son."

Ty might have worried they were overcompensating after he'd come out, but Craig's family had always been like this. The only real difference since he came out was that Mama made his favorites for dinner more often.

"Good to see you too, Gio."

Mama drew him away. "How are you doing? Are you eating enough? You're too skinny." Her scrutiny made Ty feel like a bug under a microscope. Craig's younger sister, Jenny, must have noticed his deer-in-headlights expression, since she rescued him immediately.

"Mama, I need your help in the kitchen."

She clucked and scurried away. Ty breathed out.

Gio fetched him a drink, and the smells emerging from the kitchen made Ty glad he'd come, even though he wanted to look over those police reports. Craig had given him a brief overview during the ride to his parents' house. Not that he didn't trust Craig, but he hoped there would be more information for a historian, things that wouldn't interest a police detective.

Chatter swirled around him, mostly centered on the baseball game. Ty participated for a bit, but while he appreciated baseball, he much preferred hockey.

He fell silent and went back to contemplating the police reports. Maybe he could track down someone still alive who remembered Max. Not probable but not completely impossible. He could interview them. Maybe a neighbor. What if they'd kept something of Max's? And why hadn't he thought of that before? Researching someone who lived in the twentieth century was a completely different process than he was accustomed to.

The doorbell rang, interrupting his contemplation. Weird. Nobody rang the doorbell at the D'Amatos' house.

Mama dashed out of the kitchen to answer it. She greeted the stranger effusively for a man Ty had never seen before.

Mama dragged the newcomer into the living room. "Everyone, this is Tony Rossi. His mother, Etta, is a friend of mine."

Ty stood with the rest of the family to shake hands with Tony. He was very good-looking, with the olive-skinned, dark-haired, dark-eyed Mediterranean look Ty expected from someone with Italian ancestry.

And God, the eyelashes surrounding those dark brown eyes... They gave him an air of innocence. Jenny was going to love this one, despite how much all the D'Amato kids hated being set up by their mom.

It didn't help matters that Craig's oldest sister, Stephanie, who wasn't here today, had fallen in love with one of mama's "dinner specials". Mama was now convinced she had the matchmaking gift. To hear Craig lately, she'd been more focused on getting him a girlfriend than trying to get her youngest to settle down. But if Tony was available, well, he didn't much blame Mama for trying to lock him down for Jenny. The man was totally hot.

Jenny popped out of the kitchen briefly and apologized for her preoccupation with dinner. Ty was vaguely surprised Mama didn't try to convince her to stay out in the living room, but Ty supposed there was all of dinner for Jenny to get to know Tony.

With a big smile, displaying an impressive set of shiny white teeth, Tony sat in the chair next to Ty. "So, Tyler, what do you do for a living?"

Ty smiled back. Craig's dad had already flipped the television back on and was discussing the game with Craig. It was a little odd Tony wasn't trying to make nice with Jenny's family, but since both he and Tony were the outsiders today, Tony probably found him a little less intimidating.

"I'm a history professor at the university."

Tony's grin got wider. "No kidding? I'm a high-school teacher. Economics."

Economics? Blech. Oh well, a lot of people found Ty's profession dull too. He and Tony commiserated a bit on the hopelessness of some students and applauded the rewards of teaching. Ty didn't know how well a high-school teacher would mesh with the odd hours Jenny put in as an interior decorator, but they'd work it out.

"What's your specialty?" Tony asked.

"Medieval Europe. Although right now I'm researching a local artist who died in the thirties."

"Someone famous?"

"No. But he's a fascinating subject."

Before he knew it, Ty was explaining everything he'd found, with the exception of Max's appearance in the painting to Tony, his near captive audience.

While he was describing what he'd gleaned of Max's personality, work, and family from his research, Mama emerged from the kitchen.

"Tyler, honey, who is this Max? Craig told me you weren't seeing anyone."

Oh shit. Ty looked at Craig, who was beet red and pretending to be engrossed by the game. Traitor. Like the tumblers of a lock falling into place, the explanation clicked in his brain. Tony was his dinner special, not Jenny's.

His gaze darted from Mama to Craig to Tony, wondering if any of them realized he hadn't known until this second he was being set up. Mama had never done this to him before, but Craig, the rat, clearly knew what she was up to. Tony's open and interested expression didn't change, though.

"Uh. No. I'm not exactly... Max is, uh, a research project."

Something twisted inside Ty at the clinical description of the man who was vibrantly alive in his mind.

"Oh good." Mama squeezed his shoulder. "Dinner is ready."

Craig bolted into the dining room. Like he was going to be able to avoid Ty forever. He still had to drive Ty home tonight.

Ty smiled at Tony as they both stood, Tony moving himself a little closer than Ty was comfortable with. Where had his ease with this man gone?

"You've got gorgeous eyes. If you don't mind me asking, what nationality are you?"

How unoriginal. He refrained from blurting out Canadian, the true answer and not the one Tony was looking for. It would be more antagonistic than Tony deserved, considering they'd been chatting for... Ty checked his watch. Wow. They'd been talking for thirty-five minutes now.

"My grandmother was Chinese."

"Cool." Tony gently grasped Ty's arm to accompany him into the dining room.

Well, shit. If Tony had led with the eye question and arm touch, Ty would have figured out right away and been able to kill Craig well before dinner.

During the meal, Ty developed true sympathy for the D'Amato siblings. Mama wasn't subtle. At all. Instead, she was hawking him like she was trying to convince a reluctant buyer at a used car lot.

As embarrassed as Ty was, Tony didn't seem to need any convincing. Not the way his thigh kept accidentally pressing against Ty's. For all that Tony was good-looking and personable, Ty wasn't interested.

Jenny came to his rescue yet again—he was going to have to buy that girl a gift—and drew Tony into an animated discussion about capitalism, of all things. Probably Ty had sounded as dull and obsessive when he'd been talking about Max. But the diversion gave him a few minutes to regroup and consider just why he was freaked out by the blind date. Was it that—weird interlude with Darren not included—this was his first "date" since Preston?

Tony wasn't blond. Not muscular enough. Ty wasn't shallow, and those weren't the only reasons. Tony was attractive, but Ty couldn't see dating him—there wasn't any zing. Not in his cock, although it could be convinced, and not in his heart. Tony might be a reasonably safe one-night stand, but Ty couldn't do that to Mama. She'd never forgive him if she found out.

Nope. It was Max and his hand for the foreseeable future. Fuck. Ty's face heated to boiling, and he stared down at his plate, hoping no one noticed. Why had he included Max in that thought? It didn't feel like obsession, though, more like a crush, but stronger. Until he purged it from his system, he wasn't going to be able to give any dates a fair chance.

Maybe after all the research was done, he could get Max out of his mind. Have his body stop responding to thoughts of him. But at this point, he was happy enough without trying to wedge a new guy into his life.

By the end of dessert, not only was Tony's thigh resting fully against Ty's, but his hand spent a fair amount of time down there as well. At least the guy hadn't been ill-mannered enough to make a grab for Ty's crotch. Otherwise he'd never be able to look Mama in the eye again.

Jenny began to clear the table, and Ty sprang up to help her. For the first time ever, he appreciated the D'Amatos' lack of a dishwasher. With this many dishes, he wouldn't have to return to Tony for quite a while. Jenny's mild conversation, which avoided the topic of Tony and dating entirely, allowed Ty to relax a bit, get his breath back.

After a few minutes, though, Tony stuck his head into the kitchen and gave Ty another toothy smile.

"Tyler, I'm sorry, I have to get going. Can you walk me to my car?"

Discomfort returned, fluttering down over him like a blanket. But he didn't have a choice. Not if he intended to be polite. Nodding, he threw the dish towel down and joined Tony.

Tony's car was a sporty red import, and Ty had a moment to wonder if Tony drove it to school before Tony spun him around and pressed him against it.

Tony's lips descended, and his tongue skillfully breached Ty's tightened mouth. For a brief second, Ty let himself enjoy the kiss. Unfortunately, despite Tony's skill, Ty wasn't as into it as Tony was, judging by the thick, hot erection Tony nudged against his hip.

Pulling back, Ty noted Tony's moist lips, dilated pupils, and the hands moving feverishly along Ty's arms. He could tell it was only their proximity to the D'Amatos' house keeping those hands in G-rated territory, and he was glad.

"I enjoyed meeting you. I came to please my mother. I didn't expect to like you so much." Tony licked his lips suggestively. "You're hot, and I admire your passion for your work."

"Tony, I'm sorry. You're a great guy, but I'm just not ready to leap back into anything."

"I'd like to see you again. See where this goes. It doesn't have to be serious."

But Tony was wrong. It did have to be serious for Ty. The Darren debacle had taught him that. And he couldn't get serious with anyone, not the way Max filled all his waking thoughts.

Ty shook his head. "I'm sorry. I can't. Not now."

The lustful gleam in Tony's eyes faded, and he stepped back. "If you change your mind, give me a call."

He slipped a business card into Ty's back pocket, taking rather more time than strictly necessary.

Ty knew he'd made the right decision. Max or no Max, how many high-school teachers had the need for business cards? Tony probably had more guys on a string than Preston.

Ty didn't say anything, just nodded and waited by the driveway as Tony got into his car and drove away.

A few moments later, Craig opened the front door. "Want to stay a bit longer, or are you ready to go?"

"Let's go."

Ty returned to the house long enough to thank his hostess, without any trace of resentment for the failed blind-date ambush. How could he be upset? It spoke volumes about his acceptance by Craig's family, and if that meant sitting through the occasional awkward setup, he'd do it. Craig, though—Craig earned a bit of Ty's wrath.

After they settled into Craig's car, heading for Ty's apartment, he finally spoke. "You could have warned me."

"I didn't know, I swear. Not until we got there. But then, you guys seemed to hit it off, so I thought you were okay with it. Are you seeing him again?"

"I doubt it."

"No?" The word exploded out of Craig, angry and disbelieving. "He practically mauled you at the table—don't think I didn't see his hand slip onto your lap—and you let him. You kissed him too."

"Gee, were you spying on me, *Dad*?"

Craig slumped, defeated, behind the wheel. "Ty, you talk about a dead guy like he's a friend or lover. When you were talking about Max... I've not seen you that animated or happy in a long time. I thought it was because you were talking to Tony, but it wasn't, was it? It was Max. You've been spending all your free time researching him. You're getting obsessed, and it's worrying me."

Craig hadn't spoken so much about feelings or emotions since Ty's parents disowned him. Craig was his best friend, and if he couldn't fault Craig's mom for caring about him, he certainly couldn't fault Craig either.

"Look, I know this all seems a little odd to you. And I know I'm more fascinated with Max than I've been with any other work project."

Craig snorted, and Ty welcomed the familiar sound. "It's not any work project for you."

Ty fiddled with the radio. "Maybe not. But who is it harming?"

"You have to ask that? I think it's harming you."

He couldn't believe Craig meant that. He hadn't done anything unduly crazy. "Is it?"

Craig bit his lip, hands clenching and unclenching on the wheel as he stared fixedly out the windshield.

"I've had the painting a couple of months. So what if I've been researching it the whole time? So what if I've neglected unpacking? So what if I'm not ready for blind dates yet?"

"You're ready—you're just scared."

Ty had to allow Craig was right about that. He missed having someone in his life, but he was afraid of getting another Preston.

"But you're right," Craig continued. "It's still new, and you are a history professor. I guess it's not odd after all. If this goes on too long, though, I'm confiscating your painting."

"Fine." Ty knew he wasn't giving Max up without a fight, but he also thought once he found out more, he'd be better able to focus on other things. Single-mindedness over research was not out of character for him, not at all. Craig had just never witnessed it firsthand.

"Dating too. Promise you'll be open to the idea, okay?"

Ty grinned. How many straight men encouraged their gay friends to date? "Not Tony, though."

"Are you sure?" The leer in Craig's voice told Ty he really had been spying.

"He gave me a business card."

Silence hung in the car while Craig digested that tidbit. "Didn't he say he was a high-school teacher?"

"Yep."

"I'll kill him."

Ty laughed. "Don't bother. That isn't the only reason. C'mon. Tony and Ty? We'd sound like a pair of miniature, manicured, matched designer dogs."

Craig laughed too, albeit unwillingly.

"Besides, you can take comfort in the fact that this takes the heat off you for a bit, and your mom's ability as a matchmaker is universally terrible. Stephanie was nothing more than a fluke."

The laugh was easier this time. "I'm telling her about Tony. I need all the ammunition I can get to stop her."

"Fine. But be nice about it," Ty gave his grudging consent. "I don't want to hurt your mom's feelings."

Craig gave him a light punch in the bicep that would have been a brief hug if they hadn't been in the car. They pulled up in front of Ty's apartment.

"Puh-lease! I'm blaming this all on you. You don't think I want her mad at me, do you? Now get out of my car. We'll have to go for a beer soon."

Ty locked the door behind him, snatched the police reports Craig had left on his coffee table, and headed straight for the bedroom. He stripped off the dress shirt and pants he'd donned for his evening at the D'Amatos and leaped onto the bed, wearing only boxer briefs.

"Max, since you've never had Mama D'Amato's ziti, you don't know what you're missing, but it's spectacular." Ty smacked his lips at the memory. "Fortunately, dinner was good enough to balance out the crappy blind date Mama set me up on. I swear, all the women in my life have awful taste in gay men. They can find good-looking ones, but that's it. If they're not completely bat-shit crazy, they're either stupid or they've got no substance, no potential for a long-term relationship."

Despite the fact that it had cut his evening at the D'Amatos short, he'd have to remember to thank Mama for trying. Ty was happier at home with his research materials anyway.

It didn't take as long as he'd thought to skim through the photocopies

Craig had brought.

"Craig was right. There's not a lot here. Looks like Arthur Cook reported you missing after you failed to make a lunch date, and he was told you'd up and left town."

With the little Ty had discovered, he'd be suspicious of that explanation too. Even if Max had felt compelled to leave because of Victor's increasing advances, there was no reason for him not to let Arthur know where he was going.

"I'm assuming Arthur Cook is the mentor you mention in your journal." It wasn't a difficult deduction, since the man's occupation and place of work, the Ontario College of Art, were listed clearly in the report.

"I can't tell if Grant or Stavers would have cared enough to report you missing, not if they agreed with Victor's statement." How awful. To have no one left to care. No one to wonder if you were okay, help out if you were sick.

Ty looked up at Max. The air of sadness surrounded the painting again, but there was something else too. Ty didn't know what it could be, other than his own insanity, yet he felt perfectly sane.

"Craig, of course, wouldn't want to accuse the police of complicity in a crime, even nearly eighty years after the fact, but he seemed unconvinced the police had uncovered everything. I bet Stavers knew what happened to you. I bet he's the one who boxed up your stuff. But did he box it up knowing you were dead?"

Reading Stavers' short statement again, he thought not. "He says Victor told him you'd left. Obviously, I'll never know for sure, but I think if he thought you were dead and Victor had killed you, he'd have destroyed your stuff, not packed it away in a box. I think he believed you were coming back."

Whether Craig thought the investigation was intense enough, the police hadn't found Max's personal effects. The journal alone should have been enough to prompt a closer look at Victor. But if the police had put it into evidence, then Ty wouldn't have it in his possession now.

"I wonder what Stavers thought of you in this painting."

Max grimaced. Stavers probably did think Victor had told the truth. At first. But he'd come into Victor's room more than once and stared at him. Studiously keeping his eyes on Max's face, naturally. Stavers did not bend that way. He knew Stavers had begun questioning that original conclusion as the years went by. Not that it would have mattered. The Depression raged on into WWII. Neither had adversely hit Victor's pocketbook, but he complained at length about the other problems accompanying both. Stavers had other things to worry about, and Max didn't blame Stavers for being afraid of what would happen to him should Victor have been arrested. Not that there was any proof because Max wasn't actually murdered.

"Anyway," Tyler went on. "I think Victor was rich enough and you were, unfortunately, insignificant enough that the police couldn't do much without your body or more evidence."

True. Max had been one small step away from transient. He hadn't been under Victor's sponsorship long enough to become a big name, assuming he could have been one.

Tyler sighed. "I was hoping to interview people in this report, but there's not a lot of information and I doubt they're still alive. Craig said he got the impression that the investigating officers would have been glad to arrest Victor for anything, but there wasn't enough evidence."

Craig was a good judge of character if he'd gotten that simply from reading the police reports. Max remembered the officers' harassment well. They did try. None of them approved of Victor, but without a body and without a wealthy advocate working on Max's behalf, they'd finally had to let the matter drop. But he knew all about this. Was Tyler going to finish reading that racy mystery he'd started? Max was more interested in fictional crimes—and sex.

He also might want to hear more about this blind date. He couldn't believe Craig's mother had tried to find a date for Tyler. A male date. Max was amazed, envious, that some people were so accepting. But he hated any man Tyler could get involved with. He didn't know how he'd stand it when Tyler found himself another boyfriend or lover.

Tyler set the file folder on the desk and turned out all the lights except for the soft yellow one at his bedside. He climbed into bed, on top of the covers, and somehow blood pounded in Max's ears as the bulge in Tyler's underwear grew. Oh yes. Tyler was not ready for sleep, and this was better than reading aloud.

Underneath Max's gaze, Tyler slipped his briefs off and began stroking his cock, unabashedly staring at Max.

Max's incorporeal body mimicked the light-headedness he'd always experienced when blood rocketed into his groin. This time, he fought the canvas with everything he had, struggled and pulled, kicked and hit. He swore he'd punched both arms right through it. Could Tyler see? Wasn't the canvas rippling? Throwing his head back, he yelled, veins in his neck popping and throbbing.

Exhausted and sweaty, he sagged against the canvas, almost amazed he still had an erection. But he'd have to be dead not to respond to Tyler.

"Oh, Max, I'd rather do this than go out on a blind date any day."

Thank God.

CHAPTER NINE

September 26, 1937

It occurs to me that I've been alarmingly frank in my ramblings. This place is almost idyllic in that I feel like I'm normal and accepted, even though Victor's presence does nothing to make me feel safe. However, I don't fear the law here, I fear Victor losing patience with my gentle rejection of his increasingly less subtle advances. Regardless, I will have to be sure to rip out all but my sketches and burn those pages when I move on from here.

Ty gasped aloud. This more than anything suggested Max had not left Victor's estate of his own free will, and more than likely proved he was murdered. Tears welled up in his eyes. The whole fear of the law and fear of being ostracized... Ty didn't know if he could live like that. It had been hard enough losing his parents over his sexual orientation. If he couldn't be himself with his sister and his friends, he might have lost his mind.

October 8, 1937

I met Arthur for lunch today, as I do every other Friday. I think he was concerned, having second thoughts about me working for—as he called it—a devil worshipper. Victor's mystic symbols and furtive Thursday evening outings are, quite frankly, less of a bother than the constant attempts to lure me into his bed. I've never been in love. I never expect to be, although until I lost my family, I never realized it was something I wanted. Society won't allow it, not openly, and Victor won't be able to give it to me. Neither could Grant. But Victor is overwhelming sometimes. I feel like he wants to conquer me, own me like a toy or a whore. I need to be able to live with myself, and maybe that means being alone.

I didn't tell Arthur any of that. I still have to eat, and Victor's constant attentions are preferable—for now—to starving. As yet, he has not made the ultimatum I've been expecting for days: yield or lose my position. I don't know if I'd put my principles and desires ahead of my room and board. I am very much afraid I will give in if Victor demands.

Excitedly, Ty scrabbled through his notes and the police reports. He also checked a reference site online. He sat back, thrilled at this corroboration. Based on this entry, Max should have had met Arthur for lunch on November fifth, the day before Arthur reported him missing. Stavers had told the police Max had left the estate on October thirty-first, while he'd been away.

October 28, 1937

Victor is driving me crazy. He keeps trying to get me into bed, and I can see how much it upsets Grant. I don't think Grant's in love with Victor, but he wants to be in Victor's bed, and I don't. Victor's around a lot—more and more with every refusal I give him. Watching. Tempting me with money, gifts. I don't need gifts, and I'm not a whore. I'd just like some stability, the chance to start a new career, wait out the depression. Start again. I think the best way to reduce these complications in my life, let me get back to the art without distraction, is to figure out how to turn Victor's attention to Grant. I think I might know how.

Victor has one of his occult events on All Hallows Eve. That might provide the perfect opportunity.

Halloween. Ty knew in his gut that Max had been killed on Halloween. Either the plan he'd been hatching had backfired or Victor had been deeper into the occult than anyone realized and Max had fallen victim to some sort of sacrifice.

Ty got up and stared at the painting again. The occult connection seemed too fanciful, but he'd never fully explored the odd pendant hanging around Max's neck. Maybe that was the next avenue of inquiry, even though he should be satisfied with what he'd learned thus far.

Ty reeled into his bedroom, slightly tipsy from the drinks Wendy had insisted on buying him, as though she could sense Ty was holding something back. He'd called her as soon as he realized the necklace might be worth looking into, and she'd insisted on meeting at a pub in order to tell him what she'd found.

"Oh, Max, you would not believe what I had to do to find out about this."

Ty held up the photo he'd printed of the pendant painted on Max's neck. If only research worked like it did on television. He could pull up some arcane search engine, type in a couple of vague descriptors, and bang!

There'd be one result with exactly the item he was looking for.

"Remember my friend Wendy? She teaches classical history—Greeks and Romans, but she also has background in Mesopotamia. I thought if anyone might be able to help identify this, it would be her. It took her a week to track it down, but she got it." Ty grimaced. "I had to set a date for a housewarming party, though, in order to get the information. She was hoping for Labour Day weekend, but I smacked that down. I can't be ready to host a party in a week, that's crazy. So, it'll be the weekend after. You'll get to meet all my friends."

Ty blinked a little, feeling as though the two Cosmos he'd drank had sent him meandering. "I forgot to tell you, Max. Although maybe you already know. Your pendant is an as yet undeciphered ancient Sumerian symbol. Wendy said it might even be an original artifact. I thought she was going to throttle me when I said it was merely a painting and I had no idea where the original was."

If Ty had to guess, though, he'd bet it was either hidden somewhere in the mess of Victor's estate or buried with Max's body. But he'd tell his sister to be on the lookout. It might be one of the more valuable pieces if she could prove provenance.

"Apparently, certain branches of the occult have appropriated the symbol as a source of 'mystical' power. I wonder if Victor made you pose with it, or if he had it painted on you later. Still, kind of cool to know."

But like much of what he'd unearthed, it didn't satisfy his burning need to know everything about Max. That necklace wasn't about Max; it was about Victor. Unfortunately, he might be out of viable avenues of research. Even with all the knowledge he'd put together, he still wasn't ready to let Max go. Craig was going to fucking kill him.

Sumerian necklace? Max had no choice but to believe the necklace had allowed Victor to do this to him. He hated to think about that night, but he couldn't avoid it—not when Tyler kept talking about the symbol Victor had chained around his neck before he'd made Max into his own captive voyeur.

It had been a long afternoon. Max had spent the day putting finishing touches on a lackluster landscape of the lake. He and Grant had discussed and decided on a plan to at least put Grant into Victor's sights and hopefully take Max out of them. Victor had an engagement in the evening, which made it a perfect time to start. Max preferred portraits to landscapes, and it was unlikely Victor would object to a portrait of the nude Grant, who was an undeniably attractive man. Victor had spent the entire afternoon hovering behind Max, distracting him with touches, dirty talk, innuendo. Max found it annoying and hoped his plan worked, because Victor's attention was bordering on intolerable.

Max's cock, though, couldn't quite understand his brain's refusal to give in, and as a result, he was perpetually hard, even though he rubbed off every night and most mornings. The overalls and paint apron did a lot to hide his arousal. If Victor had ever noticed, he would have doubled his efforts or bribes. Max didn't understand how he could be aroused by someone he detested, but he hoped he'd have a chance to leave the estate and seek out some uncomplicated relief once Victor was no longer obsessively monitoring his every move. He was so on edge, he could probably fuck a woman.

Finally, Max heard Victor's fancy new Ford pass by the carriage house.

Max didn't much like painting at night, but during the day, Victor could happen upon them at any time. If Grant wanted the painting to be a surprise, and Max didn't want to get in trouble for painting portraits, he didn't have much of a choice.

"Are you sure this will work?" Grant stepped into the chilly studio, wrapped in a sheet and naked underneath.

Max shrugged. "No, I'm not. Do you have any other ideas?" He didn't know what Grant saw in Victor—maybe nothing more than his money—but once Max had known how Grant felt, there was even less temptation to give in to Victor's requests.

Shivering, Grant gave Max a quick shake of his head. Even during the summer, this room was cold at night, and on the last day of October, it was positively frigid.

"Look, let's go into my room. Or yours." Either option was unprofessional, but Max didn't want Grant to become ill. "No, wait. Let's use the third bedroom. That way we can leave it set up for the next sessions. Should be warmer too." This plan wouldn't have a chance of working if Victor had a third artist he'd been sponsoring.

Grant gave him a small, genuine smile and scampered away. Max grabbed what he needed. He'd intended to store the painting in the unused bedroom while he was working on it anyway. Victor never went in there, and he was sure he could figure something out to hide it from the once-weekly cleaning staff.

When Max walked into the third room, Grant was already sprawled atop the red bedspread. He'd kept the sheet covering his body, but Max saw the erection pushing at the fabric. Covered was good for now. Max wasn't looking forward to his first sight of a fully nude, attractive, aroused male to be when he was painting instead of fucking him.

Max quickly set up an easel in the corner beside the door and arranged the lamps in the room to his satisfaction. Then he bent over Grant and began to arrange his limbs, still under cover, to appropriate positions.

With Max leaning over the bed, his hands gripping Grant's knee, Grant's cock was only inches from his face, the fabric dampening and darkening with precum. Max paused for a moment and breathed in that earthy scent, one he just loved. His cock responded immediately, and he knew he was going to find out what it was like to paint while he had a full erection.

The door banged open, hitting Max's easel and sending it flying.

"What the fuck is going on in here?"

Max had never heard Victor sound so vicious. He carefully let go of Grant and turned around, hands out in supplication.

"Victor...Mr. Cranston...I can explain."

"Oh, your cocks are doing plenty of explaining for you, you ungrateful assholes." Victor was spitting as he literally choked on his words. His face was purple, his eyes wide. He cried out, an inarticulate, angry sound, followed by throwing lamps and books about while hurling inventive yet hateful epithets...at Max and only Max. He didn't know if that was because Grant had skedaddled before Victor's tantrum had a chance to get going, or because Victor only cared about what he saw as Max's betrayal.

Dodging missiles, Max hoped Victor would calm down enough to let him explain. Otherwise he was going to lose his position.

A flying book clipped Max on the temple, and Victor faded to black.

When Max awoke some unknown time later, he was cold, woozy, and unable to move his arms.

"Help," he whispered.

Victor loomed over him. Max had been out long enough for Victor to don a black robe trimmed with red and silver. "Oh. You're finally awake."

Broken bits of memory returned, Victor's crazed fit appearing as though a dream.

"What... Victor, I can explain." His voice didn't sound like his own.

"You don't need to. Grant did. But if you're going to give me the same story he did, I don't believe it. You were going to give him what should be mine."

"No." *Mein Gott.* How had he never realized thwarting Victor could be dangerous? He should have just given in weeks ago. "My hands."

"Yes, I know. I tied you down."

"Why?" But he knew. Victor was going to take what he wanted, take it by force. And Max was too groggy to prevent it.

Victor smiled gently, as though he weren't completely mad, and stroked Max's naked cock.

Which explained the chill. Victor had undressed him as well as tied him up. And he was apparently recreating the scene Max had tried to set up with Grant, because they were still in the third bedroom of the carriage house. The scent of must wafted to Max's nose from the red bedspread.

Max's traitorous cock rose up at the attention of someone's hand other than his own. Stupid bastard. Victor would think Max was okay with this treatment. And he wasn't.

"Good boy," Victor whispered. His hand left Max's hardening dick to pull a chain with a pendant on it out of his pocket. He clasped it around Max's neck, the stone even colder than the room.

Victor grabbed his dick again and started pumping while muttering something in another language.

Abruptly, Victor let him go just as Max was getting close to coming, and the stone at Max's neck flared icy and hot at the same time.

"Oh, perfect. You'll make a better masterpiece than Grant ever would. And this is a much better punishment for your betrayal."

Peering at Max's throat, Victor frowned and pressed a finger to the necklace. Which was when Max realized he could no longer sense Victor's touch. Or smell the disuse on the bed below him.

"Too bad the pendant's trapped in there with you. But I know just where I'm going to keep you."

"Victor, stop this. Let me go."

Victor ignored him as though he hadn't said a word. Max hadn't known what Victor had done to him until Victor carried the painting—Max's painting—into the main house and hung him at the head of Victor's bed.

Lucky Grant had only been dismissed from Victor's employ.

Ty spent the last week of his break getting his apartment properly set up so he'd be ready for his enforced housewarming party. Everything was just about perfect by Saturday morning, so he had almost the entire Labour Day long weekend to do whatever he wanted, and what he wanted was crazy but that didn't stop him. Most of Saturday afternoon and evening he spent online, researching the occult and where it intersected with ancient Sumer. He knew it wouldn't tell him anything about Max, but it would be interesting to know what Victor thought he could gain by having the pendant or giving it to Max. Grasping at straws, maybe, but he couldn't let it go. He'd assumed that the end of the research meant the end of his treating Max, the painting, like a friend and companion; but he couldn't let Max go. Didn't want to. And that meant, for the sake of his friends and family, the research had to continue, no matter how tenuous the connection.

Just when his stomach began protesting how long it had been since his late breakfast, someone knocked at his door. Huh. He wasn't expecting anyone, and whoever it was had been buzzed in by someone else.

Ignoring it, Ty clicked into another web site. But the knocking became more insistent, more distracting. With a sigh, he stood and left the comfort of his bedroom.

When he opened his apartment door, Ty wondered if he was hallucinating. "Why are you here?"

Ty looked dispassionately at his ex-boyfriend. He'd managed to avoid seeing Preston in person since he'd dumped the cheating bastard. Now he didn't know why he'd cared. The artfully mussed dark hair and soulful brown eyes were artificial and contrived instead of sexy. Preston didn't have a sincere bone in his body, except for the bone that sincerely wanted to fuck every guy on two legs. Rather like Victor. Ty wasn't falling for Preston's nonsense again. He wasn't.

"We belong together, Ty-Ty."

That stupid nickname brought a snarl to Ty's lips. "What—your current boyfriend isn't as stupid as I was? Did Jeffrey see through your cheating ass already?"

"No!" Preston sounded truly offended. Well, Ty had intended to be offensive; he just couldn't tell which part of his comment had pissed Preston off. His ex wasn't stupid, though, and his expression changed to pleading. "Come on, Ty-Ty. Please let me explain."

Oh, whatever. Preston could explain until the sun went supernova; they weren't getting back together. But if he let Preston say what he had to say, maybe he'd go away. For good.

"Fine. Come in. But stop calling me Ty-Ty." Tyler opened the door farther.

Preston glanced around, gaze finally lighting on the new couch. "Nice apartment. Why'd you move? Why'd you get a new couch?"

Ty's cheeks heated. No way was he going to tell Preston his reasons, his desire to eradicate evidence of his idiocy. Too embarrassing, since Preston shouldn't and wouldn't be affecting his life anymore.

"It was time for a change." Ty was proud of how bland his voice sounded.

"I bet we could go to town on that." Preston ran his fingers suggestively along the back of the couch. "Looks sturdy."

Ty stared. Was he serious?

"Preston. We're not getting back together. We're not having sex. Ever again."

"We made some good memories on your old couch."

"I left it in a dumpster behind my old building. Why don't you go and see if it's still there?" Something occurred to Ty, making him a little uncomfortable. "How did you find out where I live?"

"Jeffrey found out for me." Preston began to—there were no other words—massage the back of his couch.

"Jeffrey?" Assholes. Ty should have known. But why would any guy provide information so his lover could stalk his ex-boyfriend? "You two deserve each other."

Preston's eyebrows rose. "I deserve you."

"I think you should leave now." What Preston did or thought no longer concerned him. Too bad he wasn't sure if the emotion left behind was relief or grief.

"You can't mean that. We were good together."

"Apparently not. If we were, you wouldn't have cheated on me." With every willing body he could find.

Preston shrugged. "Diversions. That's all."

Diversions. The man was completely deluded. Ty shook his head. "I'm done. We're done."

Preston smiled at him, reminding Ty of better times. Times when Preston was able to weaken his knees and make him tremble with little more than a touch. A niggling voice spoke up inside his head. Could their relationship be salvaged? Could he forgive Preston?

No. No way. Ty muffled that little voice into silence. Preston hadn't even confirmed if he'd broken up with Jeffery.

While Tyler considered those thorny questions, Preston walked into the bedroom. Out of habit, Ty followed.

"I like the picture."

Of course he fucking did.

"But, Ty-Ty, the uptight guy I know wouldn't buy this. You had to have gotten it knowing I'd be back. See, this proves my point. We belong together."

Preston flipped open the top two buttons of his shirt, then grabbed Ty's face, bringing him in for a kiss. Automatically, Ty complied, his body used to Preston's demands.

Preston forced his lips open with an insistent tongue while he placed his palm over Ty's cock. Ty pushed him away, their mouths separating with a wet slurp.

"What?" Preston asked even as he unbuttoned his shirt farther.

Ty glanced at Max. "This isn't what I want."

"What is the matter with you?" Preston glared. "You're such a fucking uptight prude. I liked hanging out with you, but I only got some variety on the side because I needed something a little more exciting, you know, sex-wise."

If Ty's ears could have flattened like an angry cat's, they would have. "I'd like to think whomever I end up with won't run the risk of being bored in my damn bed. And since you think that, you can get the hell out. I never wanted you here in the first place."

Preston's face flushed in anger. He grabbed Ty and threw him down on the bed.

Ty avoided Preston's subsequent lunge, rolling out from under him.

"What the hell? Do I need to call the cops?" Ty kept his arms braced for another approach as Preston righted himself and faced him again.

"You know you want it. I bet you haven't been laid since we broke up." Preston sneered. "Jeffery thought if I was nice to you, you'd take him back as TA."

A furious flush burned Ty's cheeks. "Oh, *Jeffery* thought you were so good in bed that I'd risk getting a disease from a man incapable of discretion or restraint? And it would make me putty in your hands? Don't be ridiculous. Does he even know you're here?"

A ferocious frown marred Preston's features. "No one turns me down."

"Really?" Ty couldn't keep his incredulousness out of his tone. Seriously? Never? Preston was good-looking, but he wasn't some sort of dating prodigy. Or sex god. Not by a long fucking shot.

Preston's lip curled. Braced for another attempt to roll him into bed, Ty was not prepared for a fist striking him in the jaw. Pain exploded in his face, and without conscious direction, Ty slammed a punch into Preston's stomach.

"Leave. Now." Ty had never been so angry. Or humiliated.

Preston curled up on himself and coughed, a breathy, labored sound.

Calling the cops... People at work might find out. God knows what that damn Jeffrey would think. If nothing else, he needed to call Craig, but maybe not right now.

"Bitch," Preston wheezed out.

Using Preston's partially unbuttoned shirt, Ty propelled him out of the apartment and hopefully out of his life.

"Don't come back, Preston. Or I'm going to have you arrested."

He'd tell Craig about the incident, but he suspected Preston would learn to live with the disappointment of being rejected by Ty. And Jeffery would have to get off his lazy ass if he wanted a good review from Dr. Carscadden.

Door securely locked and bolted, the adrenaline beginning to fade, Ty slunk back to his bedroom and slumped on the bed, gaze on Max.

As he pressed his fingers gently over his tender jaw, Ty's vision of Max blurred through the haze of tears. Had Preston always been contemptuous of Ty and he'd never noticed?

"I don't understand, Max. Is there no man out there who could be faithful? Am I such a fool for clinging to the hope of a man who'll love only me?"

Ty moved toward Max. He already knew there was at least one man who felt the way he did. Unfortunately, he'd been dead for decades. He was in love with a dead man, and it hurt a million times more than the lancet-sharp pain of discovering Preston's infidelity.

Tears sped unchecked down his cheeks as he approached Max and looked him in the eye. "I want a man like you. Why is that so unreasonable?"

Hiccupping, Ty knew he was lying. Deceiving himself was pointless when there was only Max to witness his misery. He didn't want a man like

Max...and he didn't know how to make these feelings go away.

"It's stupid and pathetic and completely, utterly useless, but I love you, Max. I wish you were here with me now."

Closing his eyes, he pressed his lips to the painted facsimile of what he truly wanted to feel.

And found himself with an armful of naked, muscular male—kissing him back with breathtaking fervor. Ty stumbled back in shock, and the living, breathing version of the man in his painting stared back at him, lips parted, eyes glittering with surprise, lust, and a warmer, sweeter emotion.

Heart galloping at an alarming rate, Tyler wasn't sure whether he was hallucinating. Words tumbled through his brain, but his vocal cords had forgotten how to release them.

"Tyler."

He had to be imagining the deep, rumbling voice making his cock twitch. Had to. And was that the faintest hint of an accent? How sexy was that?

Max—Max?—reached for him, and Ty stepped farther back. How had this duplicate to the man in his painting appeared in his apartment? Ty must seriously be losing his mind. More than before.

"Wait. Wait a minute." Ty glanced behind the golden-skinned man. The painting now displayed only bedclothes and shackles. Max, the painting, was gone. But Max, the man, was in front of him.

"What's going on?" Ty might be ashamed of the way his voice squeaked, but he was too weirded out to bother.

The man before him was pale, breathing shallowly, and kept rubbing at his arms like he had some sort of compulsion. But he never took his gaze off Ty's face. "I don't know exactly where to begin."

Like Ty cared. "Just begin somewhere. Because you're freaking me out, and I'm really close to calling the cops." Again.

Ty snatched a pair of sweatpants from the clean laundry basket. "Here, put these on. You're distracting me."

Max obeyed, but not before Ty got a peek at the vaunted equipment in its quiescent state for the first time. Didn't look like the painter had exaggerated any, but there was only one way to be sure.

No. Ty pinched himself. No way was he thinking about having sex with this stranger. Not a chance.

The hunger in the stranger's eyes made Ty nervous. Mostly because it fired his blood, tempting him rather than frightening him.

Ty's gaze jumped from the chair to bed. "Out in the living room. I can't..." He couldn't even finish his damn sentence. He couldn't discuss this here, with a bed nearby. Not with the half-naked twin of the guy who'd populated his fantasies for weeks now. Not with the spitting image of the guy he'd fallen in love with.

The stranger nodded and made a gentlemanly gesture for Ty to lead the way. Ty shook his head, and he complied, leaving Ty's bedroom. Relieved the stranger was being agreeable, Ty followed without any hesitation. Maybe it would have been smart to call the cops, barricade himself in the bathroom, but he didn't feel threatened.

"I'd wondered what the rest of your apartment looked like. It's nice."

Ty opened his mouth, standard banal reply ready to fall out, before he clamped his jaw shut. This was not a normal social situation. The niceties did not have to be observed.

"Sit." Ty pointed at the couch, and the other man sat.

He started with his hands neatly folded in his lap but quickly graduated to petting the couch, jogging pants, and lamp cord.

Resolutely ignoring the bizarre fidgeting, Ty wrestled the armchair around to face the guy. He should call the cops, or Craig, at least, but Preston made him more uneasy than this guy. And he knew without a doubt he had no weapons hiding anywhere.

Settling into the chair, Ty fixed his gaze on the attractive face in front of him. "Okay. Talk."

"Tyler. You're gorgeous."

God. What was it about his voice that hit Ty right in the belly? He forced himself to be stern, as though he were talking to one of his flightier students. "That's not what I want to hear."

Lies. He wanted to hear nothing else, but not right now.

"I know. But I can hardly believe I'm here...you're here, right in front of me."

Those strong hands slowly reached for him again, but Ty shook his head. "Talk."

The blond man stared at the hands once again clasped in his lap. "The explanation sounds...mad. I can't imagine how you could believe me. I wouldn't believe it, I don't think."

Ty didn't know if he was supposed to hear those last whispered words. "I don't care. Tell me." As much as Ty wanted to believe this was, miraculously, Max in his apartment, living and breathing, he knew it was impossible.

"I'm Max Friedland."

Ty's heart thumped in happiness, but logically, he couldn't, wouldn't let himself be swayed. "Why should I believe you? That's crazy. Impossible." Fulfillment of his wildest dreams and desires. Which was only one of a million reasons why this guy had to be lying.

Max flipped his blond hair out of his face and gazed intently into Ty's eyes. God. He'd dreamed about the exact same look in those blue eyes. How he wanted to believe.

"I know what it sounds like. But Victor trapped me in that damned canvas. Cursed me. Naked, for God's sake. All I did was turn him down, dammit."

Victor? If this guy was acting, he'd learned his role well—a stellar job.

Max's mouth snapped shut for a moment. "No, maybe that's not right. He caught me with Grant, and he was jealous, insanely so."

Wow. The guy was good. He comfortably threw around names that weren't readily available to the public. Tyler tried to focus on that, rather than consider how jealous he was listening to Max talk about some other man. He'd never cared this much about Preston. He also hadn't ever felt this trembling, urgent desire for anyone, not when they were both mostly clothed and hadn't done more than kiss.

"I was going to paint Grant—nude—to entice Victor. But Victor surprised us and never gave me the chance to explain."

Ty hopped to his feet and began to pace to avoid succumbing to his ever-increasing desire to give in, to touch, to find out how it felt to kiss Max when he wasn't about to have a panic attack. Especially now that he knew Max hadn't been getting it on with...some other man who'd been dead for decades too. Except Max wasn't dead. Wasn't murdered. Was, in fact, sitting on Ty's brand-new couch.

"Go on." Ty tried not to look at the man, but he failed more often than not.

Max spoke quickly and intently. Every detail Ty had uncovered thus far, Max knew, and then some. Even if he'd been spying on Ty, why would he bother to go to such elaborate lengths? It didn't seem worthwhile to pretend. There was not an end game Ty could see. And it had taken Ty weeks to unearth this information, from several sources, including the journal that hadn't been available to anyone until Ty got his hands on it. Why would anyone go to that trouble to pull a prank like this on him?

"Why aren't you as freaked out by this as I am?"

Max shrugged. "I've been watching, waiting, hoping to be freed from my prison for decades, although I never imagined anyone would actually do it."

Tyler's breath sped up, and he forced himself to breathe slowly and regularly. Hyperventilating was the last thing he needed now.

"Do you have questions? I mean, the technology and..." Ty sighed. Somehow, he'd already accepted what Max said, or he wouldn't have assumed Max didn't have any knowledge of current events. Or maybe he'd shot right past eccentric into stark raving mad.

Max blinded him with a wide smile. "Whatever you can learn about the world from porn or sitcoms, I know. Or at least...until about five or six years ago. How long has Victor been gone?"

Ty blinked. This conversation was fucking surreal. "Six years."

"Right. So Victor watched sitcoms, police shows, or porn pretty much constantly when he wasn't fucking his boy toys. Whatever's happened since he died, I don't know. I know I've got a lot of blind spots, but I'm not like Rip Van Winkle, and I haven't used H.G. Wells' time machine. I've been aware the whole damned time."

Ty stopped his frenetic pacing at the thought. Trapped. Imprisoned with no one to talk to, no one to hold or love. Holy shit! Solitary confinement for decades. But he was still confused.

"I don't understand. Why now? How did you escape?" Ty almost gave in and touched that soft-looking, lemony-streaked hair. But he knew touching meant he'd want those lips back on his, and he might never want them to stop.

"I didn't escape. You freed me."

That couldn't be right. "How? Not the..." Ty flushed with embarrassment as he remembered what he'd been doing when Max popped out of the painting and into his arms. "By kissing you?"

How fairytale cliché.

Max smiled again, and it was like sunshine on his face. "No. By falling in love with me."

Oh. The sunshine was eclipsed somewhat. "That's how the curse is broken?" Great. Was unrequited love more or less humiliating than Preston's cheating?

"Partly." Max's voice demanded Ty's attention, even though he wasn't sure he wanted to look Max in the eye. Not since he knew, clearly, how Ty felt. "It wouldn't work if I didn't love you too, *Liebling*."

The sun returned and brought friends to fill up the room. He let his disbelief float away in the face of Max's warm—loving—expression. Maybe miracles did happen, and Max was his. Ty had never wanted to believe in miracles more than he did at this moment.

Ty grasped Max's outstretched hand, and Max tugged. Ty tumbled into Max's lap, the impressive erection Ty had only seen in a 2-D painting pressing insistently against his buttocks.

"You're beautiful," Max murmured. Ty had no complaints about the comment this time. Max laid his lips against Ty's, and it was like a sensual bomb exploded in Max. His hands were everywhere, like he couldn't get enough of the sensation of Ty's skin.

His tongue delved deeply in Ty's mouth, and a whimper volleyed back and forth between their sealed lips. God. Had kissing ever been this hot?

Breathless and a little overwhelmed, Ty pulled back. He stared into Max's eyes and saw, again, love and caring, like he'd never seen in Preston's. He'd almost tied himself to Preston, never knowing what he was missing out on.

"You really love me?" Ty sounded as incredulous as he felt.

Max nodded, tongue swiping over swollen, captivating lips.

Ty thought back to some of the conversations he'd had with Max, the painting. He didn't feel silly anymore for the notion he'd had that a painting was good company.

One—no, two particular memories flashed into his mind. Waves of heat, only partially attributable to desire, erupted in his cheeks.

"You watched me? *All* the time?"

Max leaned in and brushed his cool cheek against Ty's heated one. The raspy hint of stubble against Ty's face made him squirm, but Max held on firmly.

Warm, moist breath tickled Ty's ear, and it was all Ty could do not to stroke his full erection. Max whispered a single, meaningful phrase, "I saw everything."

Without warning, Max slipped his strong, callused fingers down the back of Ty's pants, homing in on his pucker. Ty pushed back, aching for the penetration, but Max held off, content it seemed to rub gently as he blew Ty's mind with words.

"It was hot, watching you push your fingers in here, moving like they weren't enough. You looked over at me, and I knew you were dreaming of my cock pushing slowly in. Breaching. Stretching. Pressing in so deep you could feel me in your heart."

Ty didn't need sex to feel Max in his heart, but with every one of Max's words, the tension wound tighter. Ty's movements grew more frantic as he rocked, unable to decide if he wanted to press his aching erection against Max's groin or impale himself on Max's finger.

"Watching you, naked, with your dick in your hand, writhing like you are now. You looked at me. And then you came, spurting everywhere. I wanted to smell you. Touch you. Taste."

Max's heaving breaths didn't quite match the steady, deliberate words. His finger finally pushed in, and Ty groaned. "Max, please. Bedroom. I don't..." Ty panted between each word. "I want you to fuck me."

A whimper escaped Max's throat, and he sank his teeth gently into Ty's shoulder and shuddered. "That was close," he whispered after a moment.

Ty was also a breath away from blowing his load in his pants like a teen. And *he* hadn't been trapped in a painting for decades. Considering he hadn't had sex in so long, Max's restraint was admirable, but taking the edge off meant Max should be good to go all night long.

"C'mon, Max. Please."

Max looked drugged, his eyes black with lust, and Ty had never felt more desired in his life. Max slid his finger out of Ty, reluctantly pulling his hands away from Ty's body.

Ty scrambled back, eager to get Max's hands back on him. All of him. He wasn't ashamed to admit he ran to the bedroom. Not when Max was hard on his heels. *Hard* being the operative word.

Reaching the bed, Ty spun to face his new lover—new love. Someday, he'd strip slowly for this fine man, but not fucking today. Every second with cloth touching his body was an eternity. Ty practically ripped his clothes off while Max shoved down the sweatpants.

The sight before him almost made him come. If anything, the painting hadn't done Max justice. Max was even more tempting in person. Rough-hewn muscles, still defined from improper eating. Max might never have been gaunt, but Ty expected he'd fill out with some regular meals.

A light dusting of golden hair covered his body, with a slightly heavier treasure trail leading to a much thicker mat... Oh God. That dick. It wasn't some fantasy or exaggeration. Ty's ass clenched, and his head swam, a trifle faint from the anticipation.

The erection before him was a thing of beauty. Precum leaked from the tip, glistening in the lamplight. The head was purplish and almost angry-looking, but it was an ire Ty wanted to revel in. The shaft was thick, veins prominent, making Ty's mouth water.

"Please, let me..." Max didn't finish his sentence but pushed Ty gently back on the bed and straddled him. Max's callused hands never stopped stroking for a moment, and every touch was like an electric charge building up under Ty's skin. Max hadn't even started on the major erogenous zones, and Ty was already close to bursting.

Max leaned over and kissed Ty sweetly before he lifted up again to look at Ty's body. He reached out a fingertip to one of the sensitive piercings in Ty's nipples. Ever so lightly, he flicked the ring. Ty hissed. It hurt, but in the best damn way.

"I adore these." Max's voice was husky with want. "When they're fully healed, I want to play."

Oh, Ty couldn't wait.

Without another word, Max set his lips against Ty's neck and trailed down across his collarbone, down his sternum, steering well clear of the rings, and on to his belly. His warm, wet tongue delved into Ty's navel, and Ty's hips jerked in response. Warm dribbles of precum dropped onto his belly, close to Max's mouth, but he didn't have to wait long for Max to lap them up. Max licked his way down the length of Ty's cock and buried his face in Ty's balls, inhaling deeply.

"Max, Max, I need you. Please fuck me."

Max lifted his head, pupils blown with desire, his expression almost feral with want. "I need..."

"I know." Ty twisted enough to grab for his bedside table to get lube and condoms. If Ty accepted that Max was real, that their love was real, then they were getting tested as soon as Ty could arrange it. Or more to the point, as soon as Ty was able to let Max out of bed. Which might be sometime next month.

Ty watched, wondering if he should help Max. Max demonstrated enough hesitation that Ty was reminded he'd either never gloved up, or it had been a long, long time. But his willingness to do so also told Ty he'd learned a lot about modern sex from watching Victor in his bedroom.

A cold, slippery finger pressed against Ty's hole, and he opened right up, accepting Max's intrusion. They both groaned, and Ty jacked his hips a little, too eager to want much play. "Another one."

"Already?"

"Yes. Hurry." Ty moaned as a second finger worked its way into him, followed quickly by a third.

"Ready?" Max whispered, lips grazing the tip of Ty's penis.

"Days and weeks ago." Ty's words earned another groan from his lover.

Ty spread his legs and pulled his knees back as Max slicked up his prick. Max moved over Ty, and like fate or destiny, he slid inside, filling up a place that belonged to Max and maybe always had.

Max's arms shook as he allowed Ty to adjust. It had been a while, but Max fit him perfectly.

"Fuck me."

Max bit his lip and began long, hard strokes in and out of Ty. Ty couldn't even make his hands uncurl enough to grab at his cock. It was so good. The best ever.

Harder and faster, Max pumped into him. Ty's orgasm was close, but he couldn't quite make the leap. "Max," he pleaded.

And Max knew what he needed. With one hand, Max wrapped his fingers tightly around Ty's shaft, the calluses scraping on the sensitive skin. One tug was all it took, and Ty shot pulse after pulse. "Max, I love you!" he cried out as Max stroked him throughout his orgasm.

Still plunging in and out of Ty's body, Max swiped a finger through the cum on Ty's stomach. He brought it up near his face, sniffed at it like Ty's cum was the best thing he'd ever smelled, and then licked at the slickness. Kinda weird, but totally hot. Max bucked and grunted, throbbing in Ty's channel as he came.

Panting, Max collapsed on Ty, and Ty loved the feeling of warm, sweat-slicked skin against his own. Especially when the man was his and no one else's. Max gently disengaged and curled around him, just as Ty had imagined that first night when he'd stroked off to Max's image.

"I love you too." Max's breath in Ty's ear made him shiver, just a bit. It wouldn't be long before he needed Max in him again.

"Forever?" Ty asked, suddenly unsure.

"Forever," Max said with enough force that Ty believed him.

CHAPTER TEN

They spent the rest of the day, and most of the night in bed, making love in between talking, and getting to know each other better. Nothing Max said made Ty doubt he'd been trapped in the painting or doubt Max loved him.

When Ty woke up Sunday morning with a warm, naked body beside him he grinned and lay there, savoring the sensation. He had no idea how he was going to explain his new boyfriend, nor why they were already living together, when everyone thought he wasn't even dating anyone, but that was a problem for another day. As soon as Max woke up, they could make breakfast, and spend more time in bed.

Ty's eyes flew open and he sat up straight, startling Max into wakefulness.

"What's wrong?"

"It's Sunday. I have to go to work on Tuesday. You don't have clothes or know anything about modern life." Panic welled up in his throat as he imagined all the things that could go wrong because Max didn't know how things worked.

"Hey. Hey. It'll be fine." Max sat up and wrapped strong arms around him. "If I'd been transported here from 1937, I'd be worried too. I might not know everything, but I know some."

"Transported?" The odd turn of phrase was enough to shock Ty out of his panic.

Max shrugged. "Victor also liked Star Trek."

That was too fucking weird. He couldn't imagine only learning about modern life through television and porn, but if Max wasn't freaking out, maybe Ty could calm down a bit. Not completely though. Max didn't know what he didn't know.

"I don't know what stores will be open tomorrow, so I'd better go out and get you some clothes at the very least." Toiletries. Another key to the apartment, just in case. Shoes. He had to be forgetting something.

"I could go with you."

Ty shook his head. "We'll go to the mall together soon, but not today. I mean, I could probably find something for you to wear although it'll be tight on you, but your feet have to be a size or two larger than mine. No way would any of my shoes fit."

Max grinned. "True. I did like wearing your sweatpants, even if Craig hates them."

Oh sweet Jesus, he really had been watching everything.

"But I think you're forgetting something."

"What?" Of course he was forgetting something. Probably a lot of somethings.

"You've got a box with my clothes in your closet. And a pair of shoes."

Ty paused for a moment, and let himself feel foolish. "I'm an idiot." He kissed Max. "Are you sure you want to jump right into twenty-first century life?"

"I'm here to stay. Might as well."

Reaching out, Ty stroked a finger over the pendant that had been the cause, as far as they knew, of Max's incredible imprisonment and resurrection.

"We're sure about that, right?" One of the things they'd discussed in between bouts of incredible, mind-melting sex was what to do with the painting and pendant. Max had wanted to destroy both, but Ty was afraid.

Max wrapped his hand around Ty's, trapping the pendant in Ty's fist.

"I'm here to stay. And if you're worried, why don't we find somewhere to lock it up? Keep it safe, and don't let it imprison anyone else again."

Tension he hadn't realized he'd been carrying melted away. "Thank you. We'll get a safe deposit box next week and lock it away forever."

The painting was another story. Ty was fine with the idea of destroying it, but he wasn't quite ready to. If nothing else, the sight of it acted like pinching himself to see if he was dreaming. Every glimpse of the painting without a naked Max confirmed the curse was broken and Max was here with him.

"Let's shower and get going."

Max sat on a bench waiting for Tyler, bags heaped about his feet. It was their last stop and Max was overwhelmed. The many modern amenities they came across during their trip were impressive. Some of them, he'd been prepared for, but television hadn't been able to prepare him for everything. Everything was bigger, brighter, and louder than he'd ever imagined. The city smelled vastly different, and he couldn't decide if that was good or bad. There were so many people. The sheer influx of sensory input after decades of doing without, well, he'd underestimated how oversetting it would be.

He stuck a hand down in one of the bags, seeking his new clothing. The fabric was so soft it was almost soothing, and right now, Max could use some soothing.

If returning to his own time were possible, he'd still stay here. Ty was here, and there were definite advantages to not enduring the Depression.

Max shook his head. Money was something else he'd not been prepared for. When their first purchases had rung up to over a hundred dollars, Max was appalled. He'd wanted Tyler to cancel the purchase, because how could anything cost so much. But he'd promised to keep any questions or objections to himself until they were alone and Tyler could try to explain—the best solution they'd been able to come up with to help Max deal with the gaps in his knowledge of modern life. Tyler had gently told him that everything cost more. It wasn't as though Max hadn't been prepared for that, he just hadn't been prepared for the actual amount of inflation.

"Ready to head home?" Tyler stood in front of him, holding another small bag.

Max looked up with a smile. "I am. I'm getting hungry."

"Anything in particular you want?"

Decisions, decisions. Tyler had eaten so many unknown varieties of food in front of Max, and he wanted to try them all. But there was one flavor that he'd been craving.

"Root beer float?"

Tyler's eyes widened. "A root beer float? I don't think I've had one of those since I was a kid. We'll have to make a quick stop at the grocery store, though. What about actual food? Man cannot subsist on root beer and ice cream alone."

That was his sweet history professor. Made Max laugh. "What about pizza?"

"Mmm. That sounds like a perfect meal. You'll get the hang of this yet."

Tyler reached out and Max blinked at him, wondering for a moment what he was supposed to do with Tyler's outstretched hand. He glanced around guiltily before he took it and stood. Tyler didn't let go, though, and they walked to the car hand in hand, without anyone seeming to notice or care.

This was definitely going to take some getting used to.

Back at the apartment, after feeding themselves, Ty began teaching Max some of the most important lessons of the twenty-first century, starting with the laptop, how to get on the internet, how to turn on the television, and how to use the new cell phone he'd purchased for Max.

The sleek plastic of his new phone felt so beautiful under his fingers,

Max couldn't stop stroking it, although he didn't know how he was going to pay Tyler back but it didn't take long to figure out the fundamentals.

"And what's the number for emergencies?"

"9-1-1."

"Address?"

Max rattled off Tyler's apartment address. He also demonstrated he could find Tyler's contact information and use it.

"First rule of the Internet?"

"Don't believe anything."

"Second rule?"

"Don't click on any advertisements." That particular bit was a bit worrisome. He was happy to question anything, but he didn't want to break Tyler's laptop by clicking on something he shouldn't. But he was ready to dive into the vast information available. He didn't know how Tyler could be so blasé about it. That had to be the most exceptional advance of modern times.

Tyler collapsed back against the couch. "I'm still worried about leaving you alone."

"I'm a grown man. Over a hundred years old."

That comment earned him a playful punch on the shoulder.

"Seriously, Tyler, I'll be fine. If I survived everything the 1930s threw at me, I can handle this."

"But, but... I don't want to keep you here prisoner or anything, but there is crime and so many cars and..."

Max cut off the stream of worry with a kiss. Because there was something very important to be said. "I promise I will be careful, but I can't... I need the freedom to come and go. I spent so long trapped."

Tyler cupped his cheek, a soft look in his eyes. "I know. It's why I got you the phone and a key." And a pass for the public transit, although he really hoped Max wouldn't be tempted to use it yet.

Tuesday would be soon enough to brave modern day Toronto without a chaperone. "For now, though, we could pretend I'm your sex slave in your sex cave."

Max's words made Tyler flush bright red. "I can't believe you heard everything. But I'm not going to turn down an offer like that." Tyler led him into the bedroom with a laugh.

Ty left the apartment after another incredible bout in bed in order to put the six-foot-long painting of an empty bed into his storage closet in the basement. He returned to find Mandy in his apartment, interrogating a mostly naked Max.

"Mandy? What are you doing here?"

"I brought you that painting you wanted. I was able to get it cheap.

You're damn lucky that family's got so many hang-ups about Uncle Victor. When I walked in, this guy came out of your bedroom." She narrowed her eyes at Max, who had a quizzical look on his face.

"Why did you just walk in to my apartment? Didn't we have this discussion?"

"Didn't we discuss locking your door? Just anyone could wander in." She flapped her hand at Max.

Ty sighed. He knew this would have to happen sooner or later. No one would believe the truth, no matter how much time and breath he wasted. But Mandy and Craig... He needed to convince them.

"I can explain."

"He looks familiar. Have I met you before?" Mandy asked Max, who blushed. Ty wanted to roll him back into bed, but that would have to wait.

"Sort of. Can I see the painting first?" Ty asked.

Mandy walked back to the entryway and grabbed the canvas that was much smaller than the one Ty had wrestled downstairs.

He took it from her and handed it to Max. "I didn't know at the time, but I was getting this for you."

With a questioning look on his face, Max took the painting and peeled off the brown wrapping. He stopped breathing for a moment. When he looked up at Ty, his eyes were filled with tears, and his expression said Ty was the most fantastic thing he'd ever seen.

"How?" Max asked, voice thick with emotion.

"I saw the sketch in your journal, remember? Take it into the bedroom. Figure out where you want to hang it, and I'll talk to Mandy."

Max wrapped one hand around Ty's head and pulled him into a fervent kiss flavored with tears that ended only when Mandy cleared her throat.

"Thank you," Max said against Ty's lips. Ty smiled and turned back to Mandy.

"Oh," she said softly. "You're in love."

Ty's smile widened.

The soft, romantic side of her disappeared as she flopped down on the couch. "Tell me everything."

So Ty did.

When she finally believed him—and it took showing her the necklace and the Max-less painting to tip the scales—Ty wasn't sure he'd be able to get the pendant away from her. Having someone he didn't know handle the pendant made Max nervous, and Ty didn't blame him, but he knew the pendant would be vital to convincing the few people in his life he'd need to convince that he wasn't delusional.

Max returned to the living room, eyes reddened, but happy.

"Hello, Max. I'm Mandy, Tyler's sister." Mandy held out her hand, and Max took it and kissed the back of it. Mandy hadn't expected that. Ty grinned.

"It's nice to meet you," Max said.

"It's nice to meet you too," Mandy replied.

Believing the unbelievable was easier for Mandy—she was a romantic at heart. Craig wasn't.

"I can't believe I'm doing this." Craig set a piece of paper with an address on the counter in Ty's kitchen. "But then, I can't believe you convinced me about this curse." Craig's face screwed up as he said the last word, like he'd been sucking on a lemon. Ty was amazed he'd convinced Craig too, but he and Max desperately needed assistance—the sort he never thought he'd ask of his friend.

"I can't tell you how much I appreciate you helping me out." Max's voice still had the effect of a hand stroking Ty's balls, no matter who Max was speaking to.

"Well, I'm not doing it for you, painter boy. Ty is my best friend. You be careful and treat him right. And if I find out you lied to him—about anything—things will not go well for you."

Max just smiled benevolently, which warmed Ty because he knew that look meant Max was confident he'd never have to worry about Craig's implied threat. Not that long ago, Ty would have more readily believed in a curse than a faithful man who loved him, but he found his mind was newly opened.

"Okay. This guy makes the best fake IDs in the city. He's also got the contacts to put together a skeletal job and life history. It's gonna cost you some, but it should hold up to most scrutiny. I wouldn't recommend using it for a passport or anything, so you won't be able to leave the country, but you should be able to have a bank account, insurance...a *job*." Craig emphasized the last word. Max had already told Ty he wanted to contribute, wanted to work, which was one of the main reasons they'd made this request—this highly illegal request—from Ty's cop best friend.

"When you ask for a name, you can keep your first name, but I would recommend changing your last name."

Max developed a faintly mutinous set to his jaw.

"Why? Do you think anyone will recognize him?" Ty asked.

Craig looked at him like he was an idiot. "Not unless you plan to parade him around by his hard-on. That's the only thing anyone looked at in that painting."

Out of the corner of his eye, Ty saw Max's face explode into color. No one else was going to see that erection from now on.

"But you've been talking about your research project, Maxwell Friedland, to anyone who would listen. If you suddenly show up with a boyfriend named Maxwell Friedland, you might incite some suspicions. The same first name can be easily passed off as a coincidence, but first and last names? No."

Craig was adamant, and Max nodded his agreement.

"And we never had this conversation, understand?" Craig looked as fierce as Ty had ever seen him, and his shoulders were hunched up around his ears, evidence of his stress. Probably the first time he'd ever colluded in illegal activity, but what else could they do? Craig had at least seen the painting before. Besides the one photo Mandy had taken of it for her records, there didn't seem to be any other proof that the painting existed. Which was both good and bad for trying to prove where Max had come from.

Ty hugged his best friend and whispered in his ear, "Believe me. It will be okay."

Craig pulled away. "You're as happy as I've seen you in a long time. Years, maybe. I just want you to stay happy."

Max reached for Ty's hand, and their fingers entwined. After his extended sensory deprivation, Max was reluctant to let Ty out of reach for any length of time, no matter who saw. And Ty didn't mind one bit. As hard as it was to believe, Victor's madness was all to Ty's benefit. Craig looked at the two of them, and a fraction of his tension appeared to ease.

"When you get your papers, are you going to try and be a painter again?"

Craig was still concerned Ty had been taken in by a con artist. Ty wouldn't be surprised if something with Max's fingerprints left the apartment in one of Craig's pockets, but he wasn't worried. Ty knew Max had integrity, and Max wanted to contribute to their new shared household.

"No! Maybe never again."

Craig's eyes opened wide at Max's outburst.

"I've been *trapped* in a fucking painting for over seventy years! No, thank you. I'm going to start with a couple of computer classes and go from there."

They'd decided to tell people Max had been living in a commune for most of his life, which should hopefully explain the gaps in his knowledge. But Ty had every confidence that Max would pick up everything quickly. He was every bit as intelligent as Ty had assumed, based on his research. He'd rather Max continued on with his artistic pursuits, but it wasn't his decision.

Max tugged Ty closer and removed his hand from Ty's in order to place it on the small of his back. Craig gave them a few good places to start looking for both workshop space and computer classes while Max smiled and listened. Meanwhile, his hand crept under Ty's waistband, and a finger slipped into his crease. Ty's cock began to swell, but he wasn't sure how he was going to hide it from Craig without drawing attention to it.

Ty glanced at Max, who studiously avoided looking at him, but his smile had now become the devilish one that meant he wanted to play. They hadn't spent much time away from the sex cave since Max had been released from his prison, and both of them were anxious to get back.

"Right, well, that's a good start. Craig, don't you have to get to work?" Ty hoped he'd take the hint.

"Not for a... Oh." The tips of Craig's ears turned red. "Right. I was just going. Bring him to Sunday dinner. Mama wants to meet him."

Craig practically ran out of the apartment, and Ty locked the door behind him, not wanting any further interruptions.

Max stared intently at him, and Ty's stomach flipped. He didn't know how he'd gotten this lucky.

"Come, love," Max said, lust and adoration vivid as day in those blue, beloved eyes.

Thursday evening, Ty came home to an empty apartment. It had been less than a week since Max had popped out of the painting and into his arms and in that short time, Ty had gotten used to coming home to a boyfriend. As he'd always known, he adored living with a man he loved, but he was a little freaked by Max's absence.

He sat on the couch. Should he call Max? Call the police? Ty bit his lip. Should he go down and check the painting? It was going to be a long time before he stopped worrying about losing Max to the curse.

Sucking in a deep breath, he forced himself to start making dinner. Cooking wasn't something he did often when it was just him, but he enjoyed making simple things for the two of them. He wouldn't allow himself to worry just yet. Max had spent the days re-familiarizing himself with the city as well as attending the computer classes they'd signed him up for. Apparently the class was filled with elderly people, but that was to be expected. Max's old soul got along with the old timers just fine, and they accepted his explanation of life on a commune just fine.

Hopefully the same explanation would all pass muster on Saturday during the housewarming. Once Max had been well established as his boyfriend, then he'd let everyone know they were living together. Until then, Max was rooming with a friend in the west end. As long as everyone remembered the lies, they might be able to pull it all off.

Just before Ty was going to have to make the decision about whether to eat alone or not, Max burst through the door, blond hair disheveled and wearing a huge grin.

"I have a job."

"That's fantastic. What is it?" Ty's worries hadn't disappeared; they'd merely shifted focus. There were so many ridiculous scams masquerading as jobs. He didn't want to rain on Max's happy parade, but it was going to take a while for Max to learn and avoid all the pitfalls.

"I'm apprenticing at a tattoo parlor. Or at least, as soon as my new ID arrives."

"A tattoo parlor. As a tattoo artist?" Ty knew Max hadn't wanted to paint anymore, but tattooing had never occurred to him, even after their discussion about it earlier in the week when Max expressed admiration for tattoos in general. It made excellent sense, though.

"Yes. I started looking online to see how it all worked, then I came across a place while I was out walking that had a sign in the window."

Okay, Ty was still a little worried. "Can you tell me the name? Not that I don't trust your judgment, but let's make sure they've got all the requisite permits." Like Ty knew what permits tattoo parlors needed, but he didn't have to tell Max that. There should be enough information online to tell him if there had been a lot of complaints or whatever.

Ty typed in the name on his phone. "Oh. That's close by. You'd be able to walk to work." He scanned a few more articles. "This place looks really reputable."

Max's smile hadn't quit. "I just had to do up a couple of sketches while they watched, and then I had to get a tattoo. That's why I'm so late getting home."

"You had to get a tattoo?" Max's golden skin was so beautiful, but Ty couldn't deny he found tattoos sexy. He drifted closer to Max.

"Yeah. I guess they figured if I'd never had one I couldn't give one."

"Can I see?"

Max stripped off his shirt and peeled away the bandage on his arm. A small black dragon curled into a circle appeared.

"I love it, and I'm so proud of you." Ty kissed Max, who enthusiastically returned the kiss. When they pulled apart, Ty was already hard and breathless. "Want to celebrate?"

Max didn't have any trouble interpreting that question, but merely dragged Ty into the bedroom. He had a brief thought about the dinner he'd left plated on the counter, but he wasn't about to stop Max's eager explorations—the man loved touching and tasting him everywhere—in order to salvage dinner. There was always pizza.

EPILOGUE

Jeffery and Preston sauntered up to Ty's table. Max squeezed his knee gently, just enough to keep Ty from tensing.

"Merry Christmas, Tyler."

Ty bit back the temptation to correct Jeffery, telling him to call him "Dr. Williams". "Merry Christmas, Jeffery."

"You remember my fiancé, Preston, don't you?"

Oh for fuck's sake. The effort of not rolling his eyes was actually painful. Max coughed, covering a laugh and Ty nearly lost it.

"Of course. Nice to see you again." There was a marriage made in hell, but it was no business of Ty's.

"And who is this?" Preston wanted to know, inspecting Max and not liking what he saw.

"This is my boyfriend Max Cook." On Christmas Day, he was hoping Max would also be his fiancé. There was a ring waiting at home, but they'd inked their promise to each other on their chests on Halloween, creating a better memory to overwrite the one of Max getting cursed. But he didn't feel any need to share any of that with the assholes in front of him.

Max nodded in greeting then Jeffery and Preston stood in awkward silence before they moved on.

"Wow. They're both pricks, aren't they?"

Wendy returned to the table in time to hear Max's frank assessment, and she started laughing so hard she nearly spilled the glasses of spiked eggnog she was carrying.

"Jeffery has been making a nuisance of himself, bragging about his fiancé. I guess they were hoping to rub your face in it, but it backfired in the presence of this gorgeous hunk of a boyfriend."

Wendy's compliment had Max blushing and this time, Ty squeezed his knee. But Max was slowly getting used to Wendy's outspokenness, helped in no small part by repeated exposure to Ty's sister, Mandy.

Wendy handed them both a glass of milky fluid and lifted her glass in a toast.

Max mimicked her but Ty made a face. "I don't like eggnog."

Wendy rolled her eyes. "It's a Christmas party. It's traditional."

"Don't care. Not drinking it."

"I'll drink it for you," Max said.

"There you go. Your boyfriend is going to take one for the team."

"Well, he likes the stuff, so it's not much of a sacrifice."

Ty drank wine instead, and the three of them were rather buzzed by the end of dinner. Wendy brought them some more eggnogs, but Max excused himself to go to the bathroom first. He still worried when Max was out of his sight, but only because Max had been part of the twenty-first century for just a few months. He wasn't worried at all that Max was cheating on him with every Tom, Dick, and dentist. Trusting his partner completely was a wonderful feeling.

Max returned to the table, utterly flustered. "I just... I can't believe it."

"Tell us, we love the gossip." Wendy leaned in close. Max looked to Ty for direction, and he nodded. He didn't expect it to be gossip, not really, and Wendy had gotten used to Max's surprise over everyday things. She'd bought the commune story along with everyone else, and the more they told the story, the more Ty could imagine it being the truth. It was far more believable than a curse, that was for sure.

"I just saw Jeffery fucking a young man in the bathroom."

Ty wasn't exactly surprised. He'd known Jeffery and Preston were two of a kind.

Wendy gasped. "Not Preston? Do you know who?"

"Definitely not Preston. He looked about eighteen or nineteen and had purple hair."

Oh holy fuck. Ty stared at Wendy, who looked about as shocked as he felt.

"What the fuck is he thinking?" Ty had done his best to keep his personal life from destroying Jeffery's career—he didn't want to be seen as petty or vengeful—but Jeffery seemed determined to fuck it up all on his own.

"What? Who was it?" Max wanted to know.

"The only purple-haired guy here is Dr. Carscadden's son."

Max's mouth rounded in surprise. He knew plenty about Ty's professional life by now to know the repercussions of that—if found out—would be disastrous for Jeffery.

"That Jeffery isn't the smartest cookie in the jar, that's for sure." Wendy sucked back half of her eggnog.

"Well, of course not. He agreed to marry Preston. If that isn't evidence of some sort of mental deficit, I don't know what is." Ty thought he was entitled to a little bit of cattiness.

Then he looked back at Max, and he found the drama of Preston and Jeffery to hold zero interest for him.

"You want to head home?"

Max nodded and they said their goodbyes before grabbing their coats. The December night was crisp and cold but they decided to walk home rather than getting a cab.

After a few blocks, Max reached out and took his hand, making Ty melt inside. This was the first time Max had initiated any public displays of affection, and Ty loved it.

"Love you."

"Love you, too."

The best was yet to come, because Ty could share it all with his man out of time.

end

ABOUT THE AUTHOR

KC Burn has been writing for as long as she can remember and is a sucker for happy endings (of all kinds). After moving from Toronto to Florida for her husband to take a dream job, she discovered a love of gay romance and fulfilled a dream of her own -- getting published. After a few years of editing web content by day, and neglecting her supportive, understanding hubby and needy cat at night to write stories about men loving men, she was uprooted yet again and now resides in California. Writing is always fun and rewarding, but writing about her guys is the most fun she's had in a long time, and she hopes you'll enjoy them as much as she does.

www.ingramcontent.com/pod-product-compliance
Lightning Source LLC
Chambersburg PA
CBHW022032170626
46808CB00003B/1155
9780998180724